D0535475

Perfect Happiness

Books by Penelope Lively

THE ROAD TO LICHFIELD
NOTHING MISSING BUT THE SAMOVAR
TREASURES OF TIME
JUDGEMENT DAY
NEXT TO NATURE, ART

for children

ASTERCOTE
THE WHISPERING KNIGHTS
THE WILD HUNT OF HAGWORTHY
THE DRIFTWAY
THE GHOST OF THOMAS KEMPE
THE HOUSE IN NORHAM GARDENS
GOING BACK
BOY WITHOUT A NAME
A STITCH IN TIME
FANNY'S SISTER
THE VOYAGE OF QV66
FANNY AND THE MONSTERS
FANNY AND THE BATTLE OF POTTER'S PIECE
THE REVENGE OF SAMUEL STOKES

Perfect Happiness

Penelope Lively

HEINEMANN : LONDON

William Heinemann Ltd
10 Upper Grosvenor Street, London W1X 9PA
LONDON MELBOURNE TORONTO
JOHANNESBURG AUCKLAND

First published 1983

SBN 434 42740 3

Printed and bound in Great Britain by
Biddles Ltd, Guildford and King's Lynn

To Ann and Anthony

Chapter One

The fifth Brandenburg. Somewhere, some place, every moment, an orchestra is playing the fifth Brandenburg concerto. Violins are tucked under chins, bows rise and fall; in recording studios and concert rooms, and here in the dining-hall of a Cambridge college where a hundred and fifty people are gathered together for no reason except circumstance which is perhaps the reason for everything. They are together for one hour fifty minutes and for the most part will never see one another again.

Some, of course, will.

Zoe, scowling at the ceiling of the hall and thinking of the perversity of such places in which everything was hitched once to a day, to an hour, but is adrift now in a distant day, an unheeded hour. Once careful hands created the plasterwork of that ceiling. Other eyes have blinked in the light from that window. Through this room have passed beliefs too alien to contemplate. She directs her scowl – which indicates concentration rather than mood – to the portraits at the far end, above the orchestra. The portraits too are adrift. Their hefty gilt frames are a matching set but they wall in people tethered by their appearance to seventeenth, eighteenth or nineteenth century: ruff, armour, cravat, wig. They are left behind, these people, of no account, present and yet profoundly absent, presiding mindless over Brandenburg Five undreamed of in their unimaginable yesterdays.

Tabitha, in a frilled white shirt, furiously intent among the second violins.

Morris.

Frances, sitting with hands folded and face blank, recollecting not in tranquillity but in ripe howling grief her husband Steven dead now eight months two weeks one day.

It is for one of them, for two, perhaps for several, a moment outside time, one of those moments when the needle gets stuck, when what happens goes on happening, down the years, again and again, recorded messages of glassy clarity whose resonances are always the same and yet also subtly different, charged with the insights of today, and yesterday. Forever, people are playing Brandenburg Five.

Frances Brooklyn stood outside to wait for her sister-in-law. Glossy heaps of cloud cruised in a clear pale sky, the buildings glowed, people eddied around her. She waited, saw that the college clock stood at twelve forty-five, and looked no further. She never, now, looked further; she did not much care what happened in the next hour, or day, or week.

Zoe came down the steps, burrowing into an enormous bag

in which seethed notebooks, scarves, wallets, spectacle cases. "That, frankly, was gorgeous. Where's my blasted purse – I'll have to ring the office before we eat. Does the child meet us here or in the pub?" She stared with sudden suspicion at Frances. "You haven't been weeping, have you? Music can be fatal."

"No. Look." Frances turned for inspection, half a head taller, looking down on to Zoe's dark frizzy hair, speckled here and there with grey, at her interesting ugly face to which always all glances are drawn, into her glittering clever eyes. Small vital powerful Zoe; friend and counsellor.

"Good for you. I was on the point, once. All those bloody *nice* young, not throwing bricks through shop windows, not beating people up. Oh, I know, I know – privileged to the eyeballs. But all the same. Where *is* the child? Look, I'm going to dash to a phone – I'll meet you. Good grief – what are you doing here, Morris?"

"Zoe!"

"My sister-in-law, Frances. Morris Corfield. And here's my niece, Tabitha. Hi, Tab."

Frances, finding that useful mechanical smile, hugging Tabitha with one arm, looked at this dumpy man with pointed beard and noticeable brown eyes and saw in his expression the flicker of awkwardness that she generated now all around her. The bereaved are faintly leprous. "Hello."

"Morris," said Zoe, "knows more than anyone else in the world about – hang on – Baroque opera. Have I got that right? In other words, he's a musicologist. And music critic. Morris, why don't you . . ."

. . . join us for lunch, thought Frances, finishing in the head the sentence as one does for those one knows through and through, in depth, in totality, whose responses are learned as a familiar landscape.

". . . give me a ring at the paper and we'll have a meal," said Zoe, thinking: no, dammit, I want Frances and Tab to myself, we want to talk, I haven't seen Tab for a month and there's a god-awful week ahead goodness knows when I'll see Frances.

And Morris Corfield, smiling, commenting on the concert, thought for a moment and with passing interest of Steven Brooklyn whom he had not known but whose face and whose incisive irrefutable style were familiar from the television screen and from newspapers. Chairman of this and that. College Principal. A public man. Writer. Authority on, um, international relations wasn't it? His widow and daughter, then. Um. Handsome woman, pale oval face with the bruised look of those who grieve, fair untidy hair flopping over one eye. Girl carrying a violin.

Goodbye . . . Goodbye . . . Zoe. Mrs Brooklyn. Yes, I'll give you a ring . . .

"He's nice," said Zoe. "But not just now, I want you to myself. He writes for the paper sometimes, that's how I know him. From time to time he chucks me free concert tickets he can't use. Anyway, enough of him . . . That was smashing, Tab. I want to take the conductor home and keep him for a pet, by the way. I never saw such a delectable young man."

Tabitha said, "There's a boy called Mike Corfield in the orchestra."

"Ah. Son, no doubt. I'm famished. For heaven's sake let's go and eat."

Later, Frances drove back to London alone. Zoe had gone north, on some journalistic assignment. Tabitha was in mid-term. There was no further reason to be in Cambridge.

Or, indeed, anywhere.

She laid out her reactions to the day, and examined them. When you have been in the habit of expectation, of dangerous and excessive expectation, and when planning, fruitless planning, has been the practice of a lifetime, and when such habits are arbitrarily broken, a substitute is necessary. When you have learned finally and too late that life cannot be arranged and does not make sense, then there is nothing left but to move through days as they come, passively. Noting, simply, what happens.

No tears, today. The twisting of the guts, at points, but that is standard. A moment of uplift, once: the skyline of King's chapel. Warmth of Zoe and Tabitha. Music, of course, a torment.

She would return to an empty house, but that was something she had often done. Those who are married to public people become accustomed to returning to empty houses, to last-minute changes of plan, to apologetic telephone calls. Once, time out of mind ago, in the first months of marriage, she greeted Steven weeping and reproachful because he was two unexplained hours late: "I thought you'd had an *accident*. I was *worried*." And he had stared at her and said not unkindly but positively, "Frances, if you are going to be like that we shall be no good to each other. You mustn't try always to control everything."

There is what you intend to happen, and there is what happens. Events slip from the grasp; people, above all, evade. They set out as one thing, and become another.

The quiet, clever, successful but companionable young man you married becomes a person harnessed to a larger world, wanted for this and that, the property of telephones and unknown voices, present but subtly absent. "Duckie," says Zoe, "this was always going to happen, you know. Didn't you realise? I did. And he's faithful, I can tell you that. It might have been other women." "But I never know, from day to day, what to expect." "Be thankful" says Zoe.

Zoe, too, is snatched up by the course of events. She, too, is in the world of telegrams and not anger but irresistible forces. She cannot come for the weekend because the paper is sending her to cover a party conference; she must dash off on Boxing Day, sorry, because there's a chance to interview this visiting celebrity in London. Be my still calm centre, Frances love, she says, God knows I need one. And, in a different still calm centre, there she forever is, in the head, unreachable and unchanging.

. . . Sitting cross-legged on a mottled green carpet that is balding and pitted in places with cigarette burns, squinting in a bar of sunlight and saying, "Stay and meet my brother Steven, my brother what I told you about, him that's just got a first the clever sod. He's all right, though, he's not like other people's brothers. You haven't got one, have you, duckie? Share mine." And she pours tea from a flowery Victorian pot that will one day stand on the mantelpiece of an office in Fleet Street, a home for kleenex and rubber bands, one of the mindless things that travel with us through our lives: objects and places . . .

Places, above all, are minefields. This, the grieving learn. Cambridge, now, has been braved, thought Frances. Cambridge, where last year Steven came with me to take Tabitha's stuff up for her and we quarrelled because I thought he was coming home after and in fact he was going to Manchester for a meeting and he said as it was he hadn't really the time for this . . . Not a happy day, no, but one that nevertheless made a minefield of Cambridge, which has now been gingerly trodden.

Happiness, of course, is forever bound to place, to the physical world. We are never happy now, only then. Walking then on a Dorset hill, wind lifting the hair, and a hand, suddenly, on one's back . . . Sunlight sifting down through the apple tree in the garden at Pulborough, lying like coins among the daisies of the lawn. Happiness is out there, back there, in association with those sights and sounds, and to retrieve it is to retrieve them also, to bring them crowding into the dark bedroom at three in the morning: mocking. Perfect happiness, past perfect, pluperfect.

Unhappiness, now so intimately known, is a very different matter. Unhappiness is now, not then at all. Unhappiness is like being in love: it occupies every moment of every day. It will not be put aside and like love it isolates; grief is never contagious.

Loss clamped her every morning as she woke; it sat its grinding weight on her and rode her, like the old man of the sea. It roared in her ears when people talked to her so that frequently she did not hear what they said. It interrupted her when she spoke, so that she faltered in mid-sentence, lost track. A little less, now; remissions came and went. The days stalked by, taking her with them.

On the first day, on the morning of the first day, the day after Steven was found dead from a heart-attack in his car in the car park of the BBC Television Centre she had woken in a world that had no right to be as it was, from which Steven had gone and in which all should be numbed with her. Instead of which birds sang beyond the window and sunshine lay in hazy blobs on the bedspread. She had lain fuddled still from the sleeping pills that Zoe, Tabitha, someone, had made her take and had fretted, absurdly and irrelevantly, because she did not even know for the recording of what programme he had gone there. He was often on television. The known and loved face talked to her, bizarrely, from beyond the glass as though she were a roomful of strangers.

The sunshine lay on the bed and beyond the closed door was the day, into which she had to go. And the next day, and the next.

And this one, eight months two weeks one day on, in which she drove now into the gathering traffic of outer London and eventually into the driveway of the house.

The house which was not hers, in which she had lived by courtesy of Steven's office and from which, now, she would willingly move. It belonged to the college and they had inhabited it with reluctance. The tied cottage, Steven had called it, with deliberate irony: it shone anachronistically in a street of late-Victorian villas – a pillared and stuccoed building belonging to another time, that must once have stood in isolation amid fields and lanes. A graceful house, but impersonal in all the years she had lived there: an official home. The appointment of Steven's successor would not take effect for several months yet and the college administration had urged her to stay on if she wished, but she was anxious to go. She felt as though she were there on sufferance, as though the building itself waited politely for her departure. She had bought a house in another part of London, to which she would soon be able to move.

She unlocked the door and picked up the post from the doormat. Letters still came for Steven; there was one now, a circular from a publisher. She walked into the kitchen and filled the kettle. The house stretched emptily around her in the same silence that once, in the days of young children, she would have greedily savoured. Solitude is enjoyed only by those who are not alone; the lonely feel differently about it.

Frances had ceased, nowadays, to weep. There was a time when she was always crying. Tears came out of her in an unstoppable flow as though she bled from inexhaustible arteries. She could not see what she was doing, shuttered off by her tears, moving through a world that swam and shimmered, dripping into the kitchen sink, on to the wheel of the car, over the papers on the desk. Now, except for the occasional lapse, she was dry-eyed.

She drank a cup of tea and read a letter from the lawyer about the purchase of the new house. There was a letter also from Harry, spending his months between school and college on the continent. The stamps were Italian but he wrote, apparently, from Yugoslavia. There was no date. She wondered why she did not worry more about this.

The last letter was from the editor of a journal to whom she had written applying for a job. She had worked, on and off, as an editorial assistant: intermittently when the children were small, afterwards for a considerable length of time on a particular journal. When that job had come to an end a couple of years ago she had not sought another, relishing a period at home. She read the letter, which was polite but regretful: no assistance needed, either now or in the foreseeable future. It was Zoe who was urging her to look for something.

"You've got to. Essential therapy."

"If it's just therapy, I can't be bothered. Anyway, a somewhat rusty forty-nine year old is not all that employable."

"Rubbish," said Zoe angrily. "And you cannot sit here pining. Thinking. Whatever you're doing. What the hell do you think Steven would have said?"

"Oh, I know the sort of thing Steven would have said."

Steven gone has more controllable responses than Steven present. Yes, Steven would have said when a situation is irreversible you have got to see what can be done with it as it is. Not making the best of things – Steven never did that – investigating them. Steven never knew anything like this, of course, but if he had he would have coped. If it had been the other way round he would have mourned me, and looked ahead. Which is not callous but reasonable. And Steven was a man governed by reason.

Not by passion. "I think," she said to Zoe, on the fifth day after Steven's death, "I always loved him more than he loved me." And Zoe, piling suits and shirts from the wardrobe, replied, "You are a person who does a lot of loving. Steven had his limitations, that way. He was driven by other things. But he loved you more than he ever loved anyone. And don't *mull*," she suddenly snapped, "I know you can't help it dammit but don't stew things over. Promise me. Here, fold this shirt."

What cannot be said to Zoe because there are some things that cannot be said even to Zoe is that in bed it was always I who knew rapture, I who cried out and lay afterwards in a state of wonder that such feelings are possible. Steven was good at sex like he was good at everything but he could manage quite happily without it and he was never for one instant, I suspect, lost in it. Which of course does not necessarily mean that he did not love me but simply that that experience, like all others, had two faces. People collide in the dark; we do things together, but what is happening to me is not what is happening to you. Perhaps love is more profoundly separate than anything.

She washed her tea-cup, put the letters on her desk and went upstairs to change her clothes. The evening, now, had arrived and must be filled, methodically. Later, food must be prepared and eaten, and then a book read perhaps until sleep came, but first there must be a measure of activity, of mindless physical activity, doing things with the hands, cleaning the house or doing more of the clearing out that was needed before the move.

She sat on her heels before the crammed drawers of the old desk she never used and piled into a bin defunct calendars, brochures, garbage of twenty years ago. Her engagement diary for nineteen sixty-three, the pages of which were filled with tidy entries: dentist 10.30, S. to America, Tabitha's birthday, S. from America. The diary plotted the year ahead, carved it up and laid it out day by day and week by week. It placed Easter and August Bank Holiday and advised that sunrise on the twenty-second of August would be at five fifty-seven and that there would be a new moon on the fourth of May. Those things, presumably, came about. But Frances herself had added to this: she had added in her firm clear handwriting that on June the fourteenth she and Steven would leave for Italy and that on the twenty-second of November they would go to the theatre and that on December the twelfth a baby must be fetched from Camberwell.

The theatre we never went to, because that day Kennedy was assassinated and Steven was wanted at the BBC, to discuss and predict and pronounce. We did go to Italy but not for the fortnight that the diary mapped because the weather was bad and the car broke down and Steven wanted suddenly to get back and work. The future was as untrustworthy in nineteen sixty-three as it has ever been. The baby, though, was fetched from Camberwell, the baby swathed in an electric blue nylon blanket, asleep in a plastic carry cot, gently snuffling, the baby who was Harry.

Chapter Two

Zoe, six and a half miles above the Atlantic, hurtling forwards in time, eyes closed and ear-plugs in her ears, cruised in that shadowy zone between sleeping and waking. She walked with a man friend of hers in a desert landscape and in obedience to the logic of dreams the man wore female clothes and presently with further logic the desert became the London street outside Zoe's flat, the man vanished and his place was taken by a stranger who picked flowers that grew from the paving. She woke, detached herself from the neighbour whose torpid thigh rested against hers and delved in her handbag for brush and comb. Around her heaved and shuffled the jeaned and T-shirted, apparently semi-destitute crowd that peoples transatlantic aircraft. When I was a girl, she thought, foreign travel was not to be undertaken lightly and you dressed the part. I had a coat called a travel coat; now for Christ's sake people move around the world in their under-clothes. She took a postcard of a Chinese vase in the Metropolitan

Museum from her bag, wrote, "I have just dreamed of you in drag. Is this significant or merely Freudian?", addressed it, and rose to negotiate a passage to the lavatory. She stood in the aisle at the end of a sleazy, yawning queue and stared out of a window beneath which elaborately textured clouds concealed unacceptable depths of air and, ultimately, ocean. She said to the woman next to her, "If people in aircraft stopped to think where they were you'd have a riot on your hands." The woman, staring for a moment in hostility, twitched a bra strap and said, "Well, I always think Pan Am has it over TWA." Zoe, still looking out of the window, continued, "Mind, that could be said of life in general, I suppose." The woman, shuffling forwards, said, "Excuse me?" "Forget it," said Zoe. "Lack of sleep makes me light-headed."

An hour later, siphoned from the sky and into the maelstrom of Heathrow, she made telephone calls: the office, Frances.

"Hi, it's me. I'm back."

"How was New York?"

"Surrealist," said Zoe. "As ever. What are you doing?"

"Getting up. Having a cup of tea. Looking at the paper."

"Good. I like that. I just interviewed five police chiefs. Want to know about the urban crime rate? And a crazy politician. And a painter so doped to the eyebrows he couldn't have told you if it was day or night. Be my . . ."

". . . still calm centre. I'm not sure I'm as good at that as I used to be."

"And I'm an insensitive slob," said Zoe. "Listen, do me a favour. Come and have lunch. The place near the office. One o'clock. Right?"

She went into London on the tube, reading three newspapers,

one of which included an article by herself on disenchanted young people in a northern city. She scanned this with a scowl and discarded the whole bundle of papers in a heap on the seat beside her. For the last four stops she sat apparently staring at the advertisements opposite, a dumpy unimposing woman with eyes of unnerving sharpness who somehow conveyed even sitting hunched and bleary-eyed in the tube, an impression of furious potency. One or two people glanced at her and then away again with faint alarm. A girl who suffered from claustrophobia and knew that one day, quite possibly today, she would be stuck in a trapped and burning train, moved closer to her, knowing who would assume control of the situation. A man looked at her for some while, wondering why he found such a plain, even ugly, woman so attractive.

And Zoe, looking for an instant back, thought, thank you and feel free. As a matter of fact you've made my morning and to hell with the feminists. Not that one is going to go saying that kind of thing aloud. All the same, eight-thirty a.m. and straight off the overnight flight with a hangover into the bargain, score nine out of ten, Zoe Brooklyn. She grinned at the man. And now off to your office, chum, I've got more important things on my mind.

Such as my sister-in-law for whom I probably care more than I care for anyone in the world, bar one other. Who has spent most of her life looking after other people and must now be – not looked after but watched. Who has tried to plan and protect and prevent and has seen it all come to nothing. And is now . . . Oh, the hell with it, thought Zoe, I don't know how she is, beyond that stoical public face. Even her, that I know so well. Desperate? Convalescent? She loved Steven like people don't have any right to be loved. And in some deep mad illogical centre of her she thinks it is her fault that he is dead. That she could have planned his survival like she prevented the children falling out of windows or the house catching fire. Frances is the only person I've ever known who owns a fire extinguisher. She has got to come out now into the real awful world in which nothing can be arranged, in which fires are not put out.

And, travelling up the Holborn escalator, resting her flight bag on the step ahead of her, she saw suddenly in the mind, flickering for an instant of total clarity, another fire . . . a safe domestic fire of obstinate coke that will not burn in the Raeburn stove in that Paddington flat, before which squats Steven, poking it, spilling soot on the mottled green carpet, saying, "Who is she?"

"Frances Caradon. We were at college together. She's my best friend. Look, stop wrecking the landlady's carpet, will you."

"Mmn," says Steven, and there is on his face that expression, that expression of concentrated unemotional attention that means he has set his sights on some objective. From that moment on it was as certain as things are allowed to be certain that he would marry Frances.

Steven's face, thought Zoe, emerging into the street to battle through the early morning crowds, was not at all like mine. That always surprised me, from early youth. I thought probably one or the other of us was a changeling, dumped on our unsuspecting parents by incompetent midwives. Him, probably. Except of course that he was the good-looking one and changelings are traditionally ugly. He got the looks when they were handing them out, as our auntie Beryl used so helpfully to observe, *sotto voce*, of course, but not quite sotto enough. And Steven's face, apart from being easier on the eye, was the composed and controlled face of a public man; Steven's thoughts and feelings never showed whereas mine yelp and blaze from half a block away.

In her office, she dumped the flight bag in a corner, threw her raincoat over the spare chair, snatched a tissue from a flowered Victorian tea-pot on the windowsill and began immediately to type.

When Frances was nineteen she was rejected by her first lover. Dragging herself gradually from the misery thus engendered she had copied into her diary, " 'Man's love is of man's life a thing apart. 'Tis woman's whole existence' ", feeling as she wrote mature, tired and worldly wise. She found it difficult now to remember the boy at all, but the words, and the appearance of the diary (green leather, with a brass catch) remained in the head. And of course the feelings, the force of which could quite easily be recovered, though he who had prompted them was gone for ever. Emotions, as persistent as the landscape, seemed at times to be all that was left of the past; they rose up like spectres, saying remember me? The only truths, it sometimes seemed, in the whole confusing mendacious narrative.

She had visited her solicitor and was early, now, for her lunch with Zoe. To kill time, she wandered off into unfamiliar streets of the City and found herself alongside a large cemetery, Bunhill Fields Burial Ground, a graveyard of the eighteenth and early nineteenth centuries. It was the name on one of the gravestones that brought back that early betrayal: Paul Fletcher. But the Paul Fletcher in question had departed this life in seventeen thirty-six; hers – twenty in nineteen fifty – probably enjoyed it yet. She stood looking at the name and the white gravestones reached away all around her, rank upon rank of them, the marshalled dead locked in their different times. Seventeen hundred and six. Seventeen hundred and forty-five. Eighteen hundred and ten. Names, names, names. Aged eighteen years; aged ten months one day; aged sixty-seven years. There were huge trees brilliant with summer leaf, their dark trunks slicing down like sentinels among the tombs. All around the London traffic roared; office girls chattered past; an old man sat on a bench eating a sandwich. A notice said that Blake, Bunyan and Defoe were buried here. And, allegedly, one hundred and fifty thousand others. A silent army in the sour London soil. The thought was somehow paralysing; she stood staring from the notice to the gleaming gravestones.

She sat down. She thought how curious it was that responses such as this – emotions, even – could run parallel with but quite separate from unhappiness. I am unhappy all the time, she thought, and that is a total occupation, but some other part of me still goes on working. I still see that things are beautiful, or significant, and that prompts a feeling. I can be angry, or pleased. But all this with detachment, as though it happened to someone else. It is as though half of me were some stranger, living independently.

She wondered why happiness should be so acutely remembered when sorrow vanishes, like pain. Those brilliant tethered moments are seldom black. I was often miserable – but some kindly (or perverse) mechanism of the memory fades out all that, leaving quite other things, and hence an untruthful whole. We quarrelled, but all I have now of those quarrels is a pungent taste, not words nor phrases but a flavour: his silent back, my churning resentment.

Two pigeons, at her feet, walked in circles, their feet pink against the grey paving. Above, the trees sighed and shifted; traffic flowed beyond the railings. A discarded newspaper flapped a headline about a killing in Northern Ireland. Frances felt suddenly quite unsteady; she gripped the arm of the bench on which she sat. She had a sensation of being only tenuously connected to the physical world. In the days after Steven's death she had experienced the grey unreality of shock; this was different. Sitting in this landscape of names and gravestones, with the pigeons and the traffic and the newspaper, she felt as though her very occupation of the present was in question. She wondered if she was going to have some kind of breakdown. She got up and walked briskly to the restaurant where she was to meet Zoe, and sat alone at the table watching the window on to the street.

Rub the misty restaurant window and the condensation runs together and trickles down and there swimming in the clearer patch is Zoe, crossing the road, darting between two taxis, her scarlet coat hugged to her chin. It is snowing; feeble London snow that dies in black splodges on the pavement. "Bread and butter," says Zoe. "No cakes. Above all, no cakes." And the doorbell keeps pinging as people tumble in from the street. "I am in the most bloody awful fix," says Zoe. "Frances, Frances, I need you, love, I really do . . ."

"Hey – how long do I have to stand here clamouring for attention?"

"Zoe – sorry, I didn't see you come . . ."

"I'll say you didn't." Zoe, dumping herself down, shedding a raincoat (orange, not scarlet), looked sternly across the table. "You've not been taking pills or something, have you?"

"I have not. Nor drink neither."

"You're not the drink type. Never were. Now I could – I could end up gibbering over empty whisky bottles in a Bayswater bedsit. But you had that glassy look in your eye – it bothers me. Let's see what a good square meal will do. I bet you don't cook properly nowadays. People who've spent their lives feeding others never do when they're on their own. Unlike us spinster types. I've been known to make crêpes suzette just for me. The only way to self-consideration is to live alone."

"How's Eric? I haven't seen him for ages."

"I do love your trains of thought. Eric is fine and in Bonn so far as I know. Or possibly Trieste by now. I say – wasn't that concert heavenly? I wish I could have stayed longer in Cambridge. Tab was super. I was drooling with . . ."

"Pride?"

"Yes," said Zoe after a moment. "Pride." Her hand, for an instant, touched Frances's knee. "And other things. She had such a look of Steven, fiddling away like mad there. I mean Steven when he was that age, intensely doing things. Never letting anyone else interfere."

"She is like Steven, often."

"Nature, nurture . . . I never know how much she misses him. She never says."

"I don't know either." Frances crumbled bread in her fingers. That sensation of unsteadiness lingered still, even through the conversation, Zoe's presence. She said, suddenly, "I have this odd feeling these days that absolutely nothing is real. Not even the past. Especially the past. I can't really explain what it's like. It's as though because Steven is no longer here there is nothing to confirm what happened when he was. How we were together."

"Other people can confirm. Me. The children."

"That's not quite what I mean." Frances looked away. "It's as though because there is only me now who knows what our life was together then I may be lying about it whenever I think of it. Whether deliberately or not. I am almost ceasing to be sure myself exactly how anything was."

"It always is a two-sided business."

"I know. But this is more than that."

"I wondered how you were really feeling," said Zoe. "I didn't realise it was quite like this."

"It's not unbearable – don't think that. Just . . . unnerving."

"Don't for goodness sake be so apologetic. Be a burden, for once. By the way, did you get any joy out of that editor?"

"No. In any case I'm not entirely sure . . ."

"I am. Occupation. It wonderfully concentrates the mind."

"Stop offering therapy," said Frances, with sudden force.

They stared at each other in surprise. "Good," said Zoe. "We both needed that. O.K. – I'll stop. You're probably right. Let me try offering explanations instead. I think you feel the way you do because of a whole confused guilt about Steven being dead – all right, all right, I know, amateur psychology – which is to do with the kind of person you are. You've always thought you could save people you love. Stop the lightning striking them in particular. Remember Tabitha and the bicycle? And Steven was always apparently untouchable. Born with a silver spoon, as our Auntie Beryl used to say."

"It's a theory," said Frances, "I suppose."

"You know something? You look less glassy-eyed. I love you. Where's that darn waiter? I'll have to be back in the office by two-thirty."

In the tube, riding down an escalator, Frances studied the advertisements; men and women in the pink of health, serene and glossy, displayed underwear and liquor or simply smiled above printed promises. They bore little resemblance to the people around her – untidy, preoccupied, hurried or merely bored. The eyes in the framed faces met hers in frozen greeting; the glances of fellow travellers slid away, as though caught in an act of intrusion. From far off down tunnels came the dismal baying of football fans.

Zoe, climbing the stairs to her flat at the top of a tall house in Fulham, was stricken suddenly with exhaustion. She hauled herself up the final steps, unlocked the door, dropped her bags and threw herself on to the sofa, where she fell almost instantly asleep. The telephone, minutes later, awoke her. "You!" she said. "For Christ's sake! I thought you weren't due back till the weekend. I just wrote you a postcard about the funny things you do in dreams." At the other end, the man who had been for ten years Zoe's friend and lover made explanations. Zoe yawned. "Excuse me. I'm a dog's dinner right now. I'm asleep. If it had been anyone else I'd have bawled them out. Tell me about Bonn . . ."

Eric Sadler was also a journalist. Zoe had persistently declined either to marry or live with him. There are certain relationships at which I am excellent, she said, such as friend and sister and even up to a point daughter, and others at which I know I should be supremely bad. Let's not find out. This caution seemed, to those who knew her, uncharacteristic of a person otherwise almost addicted to risk. Zoe's provocative pieces, her public quarrels and her crusading temperament were her professional hallmarks. Eric apparently accepted the situation; from time to time he would take up briefly with other women, only to return to Zoe who displayed neither jealousy nor resentment. He lived a few streets away, in a block of flats the roofline of which Zoe could see as she sat at the window, the telephone in her hand. When the conversation was over she stared down for a while into the private garden of the square below; dogs and small children skittered among the bushes. There were always dogs and children there, a permanent and yet transient population; in the fifteen years in which she had lived in the flat children had become adults, dogs had been replaced by other dogs. The big white nineteenth century houses presided over successions of energies and high spirits, just as they enclosed shifting generations of people, a flow of humanity washing through the square. As she watched, a spotted football flew into the air and over the railings, to bounce off the roof of a parked car. On the grass of the garden a small boy stood transfixed, his panic communicating from fifty feet below.

She ran herself a bath and lay in it composing an article about the American gun laws. She had interviewed an old man who had shot a boy of fifteen, one of a marauding gang who had thrown snowballs at his car. She had interviewed also the boy's distraught embittered mother. The old man said bleakly that he wished he were dead: that flare of anger, and the availability of the gun, had wrecked his life. Her article would be brisk and loaded with statistics; it would quote and discuss and record.

What it would not do would be to reflect on the random and fatal conjunction of lives, which was not relevant to the problem of the gun laws. I should write novels, Zoe thought, novelists get to have a go at all the interesting stuff. If only . . ., that old man kept saying, if only they hadn't . . . if only I hadn't . . . If only it hadn't happened I'd be enjoying my retirement in Florida. What a lot of emotion is spilled hungering for a different past.

She lay drowsing. Oh Steven, she thought, I miss you. I'd have called you, later, and told you the gossip I picked up in New York and about that crazy Senator and had a barney with you about one of our many subjects of disagreement and felt the better for it. I don't understand death. It's not a question of raging or refusing to accept; I simply don't understand it. I don't understand how a person can go, for ever. How the air-space – for lack of a better term – that person filled is empty; how there is nothing left but a name and some unassociated thoughts. My thoughts and Frances's thoughts and the thoughts of a few others. How can Steven, of all people, be reduced to a matter of other people's thoughts?

Mum used to put us in the bath together, time out of mind ago. Taking it in turns theoretically for the tap end, but as soon as she wasn't looking we used to start a fight about it, may the best man win, me usually because I was more reckless about splashing and getting found out. Steven would calculate and manoeuvre. I was always the one in trouble. Poor mum and dad, we bewildered them from the start. We were clever and not ordinary and we burst out of their lives, perhaps we were both changelings. Mum looks at me now from behind a wall of knitting bless her and says, keeping well, I hope, dear, that's good, mind I couldn't live like you do but of course you have your job. She avoids reading anything I have written. It embarrasses her still to have a daughter who gets her name in the papers. Steven on the telly was acceptable; television confers status at least in Marlow and anyway Steven's world was more mysteriously respectable. But we were both cuckoos in the nest; we should have been unobtrusive and uneventful and lived out tidy lives in the Thames valley, like mum and dad. When dad died the neighbours turned out and said he had a good life, he had what he wanted, he always kept the garden wonderfully, he'll be missed at the Rotary. True, all of it; I doubt he ever knew the torments of frustration or envy or aspiration. Clearly genetics are not always straightforward. They gave me a good plain serviceable name and when I was seven I announced that I was not Jane but Zoe, the second name given me in dutiful tribute to dad's mother who died young. Maybe she was the errant gene. But I knew I couldn't go through life as Jane, with my face and my temperament. And because I was always more strong-willed than either of them or even both together they had to give in, and Zoe I was and am. Zoe Jane.

The bath water cooled and in it Zoe dozed, sliding without effort into that restful place where reality is fractured, where emotion is untrue, where things are not really happening, from which one can always escape. She dreamed and half-dreamed; she had sex and lost her temper and fled in fear, but none of this could touch her. She woke, with a start, to the pealing telephone.

Chapter Three

Frances, given all her life to the construction of alternative futures, stuffed into a black plastic bag the contents of those ransacked drawers – the old calendars and Christmas cards and engagement diaries. The black plastic bag would be received into the churning maw of the council lorry and the shredded remains consigned to some smouldering rubbish tip. Or so one supposed. The diary with its dead days would become pulp or ash and the days themselves would survive only in the head, a random selection. Most would be extinguished, unless they happened to include the assassination of Kennedy, or more personal circumstances whose echoes inescapably persist.

The wedding day, preserved in the photographer's album gently requested by Steven's parents (and indulgently despised by hers, people of a different caste of mind). Glossy faces smiling (or not) amid flowers and hats and the draperies of some public room. The album must be kept, though what it shows is neither what happened nor what was rehearsed, at least by Frances. Mostly, what did not happen is eclipsed by what did, but those dreaming rehearsals, curiously, survived yet, the anticipatory time during which she went to work and rode in London buses and controlled in the head the processes of that day. Held conversations and constructed scenes, considered and arranged and re-arranged. Presided over the fraternization of her parents and the Brooklyns, hopefully joined together Zoe and her friend Henry Winters, drove away with Steven into – well, no, not into the sunset but at least a rose-tinted plane to Venice. All this lingers still, but is overlaid by the sharper image of her mother and father, smiling benignly but uncomprehendingly at the Brooklyns who are enduring the day, and can be seen to be doing so. And Henry Winters was unable in the event to come and did not care for Zoe when eventually he did meet her. And the plane was tiresomely delayed so that what remains is irritability at the airport born of tiredness and subsiding elation. And Steven's briefcase, stuffed with work which surely could have been laid aside for a few days. And Zoe, later, fondly scoffing: "Your parents, love, and our mum and dad, will send each other Christmas cards for five years and be thankful never to set eyes on one another again. Our mum and dad are alarmed by yours, and yours are made uncomfortable by ours. So what? Why should everybody love each other?" – and, reading Frances's thoughts – "Oh yes, of course they like Steven, your dad can spot a young man who's going to go far, and don't think I'm being snide, he's not headmaster of a famous school for nothing, he knows a high-flier when he sees one. So Steven gets the British Housemaster seal of approval. And don't look like that, you silly girl, my mum and dad don't *want* dinner invitations and weekend parties; they want to sit tight where they feel safe and no-one's going to expect them to put themselves out."

Thus, the wedding day. Crystallised now, but susceptible of course to the revisions of what is yet to be.

Making love, at last, in the Venetian hotel, in the small hours of the morning, exhausted and with waning desire but mutual compunction. Frances dazed suddenly with the realisation that it is true, it has happened, she is married to Steven. Standing beside the bed pulling off her clothes, with the new nightdress laid out ready and Steven saying I shouldn't bother to put that on, darling. Are you sure you want . . . she says, seeing for an instant his tired face, and he answers firmly that of course he does, why, don't you? Have you . . .? says Steven delicately, and she says just a minute, I'll pop in the bathroom, and once there she takes the diaphragm from her toilet bag and looks at it and puts it back again with guilt and abandon knowing that he would be cross but she can always say it was an accident, everyone knows they're not a hundred per cent reliable. And oh please God may I have a baby. Lying beside Steven in the morning, holding his hand, water slapping the sides of a canal beyond the window, privately and indulgently constructing this child, its eyes its hair its sayings the school to which it will go its clothes . . .

Today, in north London, taking the black plastic bag outside the back door, such games are no longer played. The wisdoms of today cloud the reflection, lying across that frame of the Venetian bedroom like slides flung down one upon another. Steven's profile against the flashing poplars of a French road, swish-swish, the kilometres ticking away, another twenty-five to go, another fifteen . . . Zoe, lying against huge feather pillows, saying, "Give us a kiss . . ."

She put the plastic bag down beside the dustbins and the growing heap of domestic rejections alongside. This paring down of possessions gave her a dour satisfaction. She stood staring at the line of rooftops opposite. The sky had the immense and translucent look of city skies; aircraft crawled across it. The skimpy front gardens of the houses were shabby with London summer, offering tattered leaves and grass pocked with litter. The pavement was planted at regular intervals with young trees girdled by little wire fences, products of the energies of the local Residents' Association, of which Steven had been for some years the inactive President. They can have my name, he said crisply, but not my time, I'm afraid; the arrangement was apparently agreeable to all. The trees were flourishing, in copious leaf and unvandalised.

A neighbour walked past, smiling awkwardly as she caught sight of Frances. She had never succeeded in making more than peripheral contact with others in the street. Those who knew of Steven tended to be intimidated; those who did not were puzzled at their failure to match the house. Living somewhere like that, they should have appeared richer or smarter. Steven, in any case, was both bored and irritated by random social contacts. He was impatient with the foolish and disliked being exposed to the curious responses that the well-known arouse in others: lust, prurience, hostility and aggression. He had perfected the art of avoidance; entering a room, he would select at once those to whom he wished to talk, and slide quite unobtrusively away from everyone else. He seldom gave offence, oddly enough; he was adept at simply disappearing, not being at hand, slipping from the room. The neighbours had seldom seen more of him than a departing back and an undiscriminating smile. Frances, tarred with Steven's inaccessibility, was on equable but distant terms with them. Content with her life, she did not really wish it otherwise, but disliked the idea of being thought aloof.

In a few weeks, now, she would leave this street behind. It would become, simply, another landscape in the head. She tied the neck of the plastic bag more tightly, rearranged a stack of cardboard boxes, and went back into the house. She had to go out, to attend the meeting of a committee arranging a series of lectures in Steven's memory.

"Hi!" said Zoe. "Fred! Long time no talk to you. Where are you? We have a stinking awful line, I can hardly hear you. What? Milan. What the hell are you doing in Milan – covering the Scala season? What's a self-respecting political correspondent doing in Milan? Sorry – spell that one out, I didn't get it. Yes, I have a nephew called Harry Brooklyn."

She wrote, fast. "Just give me this slowly, Fred, and shout, do you mind. Right. Yes, I've got that. Jesus . . . Well, thank God for that at least. Give me that hospital's name again. Which lot of nuts was this? Oh hell – what does it matter . . . No, you were absolutely right to call me first. Thank you. When exactly was this? Good – I can get to her before she sees a paper. Yes, sure I'll let you know."

The sound of Frances's telephone beginning to ring was drowned by her slam of the front door. She walked quickly down the street to the bus-stop; she would have preferred to leave the planning of these lectures entirely to those involved, feeling she had little or nothing useful to offer, but people had been insistent. People she did not know, or hardly knew. Voices and names from Steven's external life; voices to whom, over the years, she had said sorry, I'm afraid he's not back yet . . . can you just hold on, I'll write that down . . . Names at the foot of letters, scrawled on memo pads.

Well, go with him, says Zoe, years back, counselling, calming . . . Go to the bloody conference with him, leave the kids with your mum, go and swan around Stockholm or wherever it is for a few days. And so, suddenly, there she had been in this glassed and carpeted hotel in which milled people docketed with their names and occupations and where Steven, similarly docketed, underwent before her eyes a strange metamorphosis. He became someone else. She saw him on the far side of rooms, on platforms, hurrying down corridors, and she saw him as a different person. His expression and his gestures lost the significance of intimacy and became those of an acquaintance. The response of others fed this process; she caught snatches of conversation – "Brooklyn of course has a personal axe to grind", "I want to get Steven on the sub-committee", "Steven Brooklyn could be sounded out on that". At night, in bed, she searched his face and found in it the shadow of this stranger. She told him that she felt, here, distanced from him, and they quarrelled, in that alien room, with light from passing cars washing across the linen-weave curtains. He said, "Frances, sometimes you are possessive", and the words, for years – still, today – stayed in her ears. She wanted to ask him if he loved her, and did not do so. The next day, she sat with a hundred others in a lecture hall and stared at Steven as he spoke: the way the light flashed on his glasses, the tiny scar on his cheek from when he fell off his bike as a boy, the bit of hair that flopped down on to his forehead, the shirt that she had washed. They had been married now for seven years and she thought of this man for much of every day; his moods and his requirements dominated her life not by reason of selfishness or arrogance but because she wished it so. He was her centre. Sitting here, in this strange city, among strangers, her own obsession seemed both misplaced and irrelevant. After the lecture people had gathered round him. She saw him locked in conversations, jotting something on a pad, turning to those who loitered for a word. A man she recognised, a colleague of Steven's from home, said, "Busy fellow nowadays, your husband, you'll have to wait your turn." She flushed, for herself and at his ineptitude. After that, she seldom accompanied Steven on such occasions. There were tracts of his life of which she knew little, alien jungles whose allure she resented but to which she was resigned. Despising herself, she envied the safely paired lives of neighbouring women. She paid bills and attended school speech days alone and read Steven's name in newspapers, often in contexts of which she knew nothing. If she asked him questions he answered patiently. If I don't tell you about things, he said, it's because I assume you wouldn't find them particularly interesting. I spent all morning with the Roland Committee. I had lunch with someone from the BBC. In the afternoon I gave a lecture at the Institute and then was nobbled by a rather tiresome woman called somebody Geering who wants me to contribute to a journal she edits. He looks across the room, smiling; in a bowl, blue hyacinths lurch on fleshy stalks and beyond the window Tabitha and Harry whoop on the garden swing.

The Institute was in a part of London she did not know. Stopping on a corner, she studied the *A to Z*. The street, in fact, was in a state of frenzied transition. On one side, a terrace of nineteenth century houses was decked with builders' signs and 'For Sale' notices; raw new windows gaped glassless, the pavement was littered with hillocks of yellow sand. Here and there a whole frontage was in the process of reconstruction – the original London stock bricks carefully replacing the demolished structure as though the houses possessed the secret of eternal resurrection, springing time and again from their own rubble. But on the opposite side was a building-site, screened by high hoardings above which cranes wandered stork-like, swinging timbers and girders against the skyline. And beyond it stood a new block, a building almost entirely encased in glass, rank upon rank of rectangular mirrors across which flowed the reflection of the sky and clouds so that the building seemed in a state of perpetual movement, swimming above the traffic and the building site and the cluttered façade of the nineteenth century terrace. This, Frances realised, was where the Institute had its offices.

There were half a dozen people at the meeting, only two of whom she had met. She sat silent through much of the discussion, imagining Steven in conjunction with these strangers; in her obsessive thoughts of him, lately, his relationships with others – and so many others – had become a curious threat. It was as though they had the capacity to dilute her hold on her own memory of him. "Sometimes you are possessive . . ."

"Are you happy about that, Mrs Brooklyn?"

"I'm sorry?" she said, guiltily.

"That we should have the lectures here."

"Oh yes, of course."

After the meeting ended she stood for a while in perfunctory talk. People drifted off. A woman who had made brisk and practical suggestions came up and offered a glass of sherry. "My name's Patricia Geering. I work here. I knew your husband quite well."

Frances remembered. A rather tiresome woman called somebody Geering . . .

"He didn't like me, I'm afraid." The woman, suddenly, smiled. Frances, embarrassed, stared into her sherry.

"Sorry, that sounds awful. I just didn't want you to think I was an old crony. I had a great respect for him. And there were plenty of people he didn't like, so I never felt especially discriminated against." She smiled again; amiable, sympathetic. Frances said something about Steven being involved with so many organisations, working with so many people. The remark sounded as inane as it was.

"Of course. And he was always a tonic to work with. If he said he was going to do something he did it. If he promised to be somewhere, you knew he would be." Patricia Geering beamed, showing bad teeth. "It was largely thanks to his fund-raising efforts that we were able to move here. This block was only finished a couple of years ago, you know. This was one of the last surviving bomb-sites." She gestured at the room and Frances, glancing at the filing-cabinets and black swivel chairs and glossy walls had a disorienting sense of the whole arrangement as a frail palimpsest upon the landscape of rubble and willowherb and buddleia that had preceded it and the Victorian brick that had presumably filled the space before that. She said, with a sudden frankness induced by the sherry and this friendly woman, "One of the most unnerving things about bereavement is that it rocks any sense of permanence."

"So I imagine." There was a moment's silence, and then Patricia Geering went on, "Incidentally, we have some books and copies of periodicals of Steven's here. I've been meaning to get in touch with you before about them. Things he loaned to the library at one point. Should I have them sent to you? Come and see what there is, anyway."

She took Frances into a room heaped with books and papers, lined with filing-cabinets. "They're in here somewhere, I know. This is the editorial room – chaos at the moment, my assistant left recently and I've not been able to find a replacement. Ah – here we are." She pulled out a box. "Have a look through, anyway."

Frances said, "Why don't you keep them for the Institute? Truth to tell, I'm trying to dispose of books, rather than acquire more. Most of his library is going to the university. I'll just take this one of his own – it's the first he wrote and out of print now." Opening the book, she saw Steven's handwriting on the fly-leaf: S. Brooklyn, 1958. The ink faded to a light brown, like old photographs.

Patricia Geering said, "Well, that would be very nice. Thank you. Let me give you a copy of the journal. There's an obituary . . ." Her voice trailed away. Brightly, she went on, "But of course it's home from home for you. You did editorial work yourself, didn't you?"

"Yes. As a matter of fact I . . ."

"I say, I suppose you wouldn't like to come and help me out? That is, if you're free."

"I am," said Frances, "I do want a job. But . . ." she hesitated, "I'm just about to move house. Maybe after that . . ."

"Think it over, anyway."

On the way home Frances thought, why didn't I jump at that? Say, yes please, next week please. The move was an excuse. I am behaving as though I were convalescent. And this job is right in the middle of Steven's territory, he would be on all sides. I'm not sure that I want that.

Tabitha, roaming the shelves of a library, came at almost the same moment upon the same book. She, too, looked inside, and saw a date which, being before her own birth, had the flavour of another kind of past - not only more distant but reassuringly unreachable. She put the book back, and went to her desk, where she sat for a while not reading or writing but with her eyes pricking. Distantly, Steven's firm no-nonsense voice told her to pull herself together and she sniffed and blew her nose and picked up a pen. When you were a small child mum was the one you rushed to when something was wrong and dad was a person whose most frequent word was "sensible". Be sensible; don't be silly. And who wasn't often there, anyway. And then later mum went on being mum but dad somehow turned into a different person, a visitant from busy adult worlds, a little alarming for that merciless common sense, but more approachable. You realised he was sort of famous, and preened yourself accordingly, and were ashamed for doing so. You smouldered your way through being fifteen and sixteen and thought you hated them both and then realised you didn't and suddenly they both seemed in some odd way physically smaller and in no way infallible and more lovable and then . . . And then it happens, the sort of thing that should be going on outside, over there, in someone else's life, not yours. So that at first, in the first few weeks, you woke at night having dreamed it hadn't really happened, he was still alive, it was all a dream.

It was real now, digested: true. Things could still make the eyes smart, like coming across that book, or getting through the first Christmas without him. And there was always the knowing that whatever one felt oneself it didn't bear much relation to what mum was feeling, and had felt. Knowledge lurked, now, of unsampled depths; the world was shadowed in places where there had been untrammelled sunlight. It was like those first childhood experiences of complexity of feeling.

. . . You belt down the road on the new bike, aged about eight, feeling ten feet tall, as brave as a lion, as fast as sound. And suddenly you look up and see her, standing there with a sort of smile that isn't quite a smile, and you are swamped by another feeling, as grey as guilt, as hot as pity. Because you know she didn't want you to have the bike in case you got yourself killed by a car, and you went on and on at them and in the end you were allowed to. And hence this feeling – queasy, treacherous – and the hiss of the tyres on the tarmac and the cold of the wind in your hair have lost their flavour.

She turned to a clean page of her note-pad and began to write. Another hour and a half in the library; finish the essay by the evening. Around her people rustled and breathed and coughed, the pervasive present. In three weeks time she would be twenty-one.

Frances, turning her key in the front door lock, heard the telephone ringing inside the house. Doggedly, like an alarm.

Chapter Four

"It would have to be Venice."

"Sorry?"

"Oh, Christ," said Zoe, "I'd forgotten. Look, for goodness sake let me jack in this damn deadline . . ."

"No. I'm going to do this on my own. I want to do this on my own."

"What's the hotel? Call me – promise."

"I promise. Tell me again exactly what the hospital said."

"Broken right leg. Cuts and bruises. Something about his shoulder that I didn't follow but it's not serious. One of the lucky ones, they said."

Frances closed her eyes for a moment. She put her hand on the desk.

"Hello? Are you there?"

"I'm here. I'd better go now – I haven't packed and the plane's at twelve."

"Swear you'll call me. And give that boy a hug from me and tell him trust him to have to be where the action is. Remember Cornwall?"

"I remember Cornwall," said Frances.

"It's nasty, isn't it?" said the woman on the plane. "Having to go to the same airport. Though in a way you can't help thinking well lightning never strikes twice . . . I said to my husband when we saw it on the news, three days later and it could have been us. One of the people killed was English. The Arabs did it."

From the seat beyond, her husband sent a prying look at Frances. "No they didn't – it was those Italian terrorists. Going on holiday, are you?"

Frances said, "No, not exactly." The Alps glittered below.

"It's our first time there. The Lakes we've done twice, and Florence. You can never have too much of Italy, I say."

The woman offered a packet of sweets. "No? I read somewhere the bomb was in one of those Alitalia holdalls. The black plastic kind. I'll never see one again without wondering. They'd stood it just by the Duty Free."

"The odds against being involved in something like that yourself are something of the order of a million to one," said the husband. "I told you that when there was the IRA bombing in London. I said, the chances that it's *you* in Oxford Circus Underground at that precise moment . . . It's like plane crashes."

"Oh, shut up!" The woman nudged him, her eyes still on Frances. "You know I'm windy about flying. On your own, are you?"

"Yes, I'm on my own."

All along the cigar-tube of the plane heads lolled. A small

child sank its chin into the top of a seat and stared backwards at the rows of faces. Frances's head ached; she had not slept much the previous night. She felt slightly unsteady and when she filled in the flight card her hands were shaking. She kept checking her handbag: passport, ticket, addresses of hotel and hospital. She closed her eyes. Beside her, the woman opened a magazine.

Over the years, one's heart had almost stopped a dozen times: leaning over a cot in which a baby lay unnaturally still; a squeal of brakes coinciding with the disappearance of a child; Tabitha delirious with fever and a thermometer that read one hundred and five; Cornwall . . .

The bright Cornish beach from which, suddenly, Harry is absent. The cliff, the tide . . . the stuff of newspaper items, tucked away behind public events. The frenzied scurrying to and fro. Zoe, with borrowed field-glasses: "There he is, the little sod, up there." The man with a rope, and the thundering relief that switches in a split second to embarrassment, guilt. Steven on the phone, matter-of-fact. Defiant, humiliated Harry.

The plane began to bump. The woman was stowing her magazine into a grip. "Down we go. Here's to the first campari soda. Staying out at the Lido, are you?"

"No, actually I'm not."

The husband, emptying English money from his pockets, leaned over. "A word to the wise. If you don't know the place I'm told the thing to do is steer clear of the guided tours. You can do better on your own. Have a good time."

Released into the airport, she saw the broken windows, the hastily erected boarding screening off the wrecked area. She walked past and out into the soupy heat.

Once upon a time a long time ago she had dropped similarly

out of the sky and similarly had stepped into a launch that had sped through the grey water trailing a white fan of foam. Then as now there had been this circular world fringed with a skyline of domes and spires against an apricot horizon. Steven had said, "Seeing this, Marco Polo seems somewhat unobservant not to have cottoned on to the fact that the world is round before he set off." She had held his hand and shed the rest of the day and sat entranced, in perfect happiness. She knew nothing of Harry nor Tabitha nor John Kennedy who would be assassinated nor Cuba nor Vietnam nor crazy Red something terrorists. Nor this other Frances who sat here now, not happy at all. She had made certain arrangements for her life which included none of these.

The launch thumped over corrugations from another wake. Someone beside her lurched sideways. "Excuse me." All the other passengers seemed to be American. This woman wore a trouser-suit with knife-sharp creases and a straw hat. Her sun-glasses poked up at the corners, giving her a cat-face. Frances thought, if I notice things still, I am all right. She had a feeling of disorientation that edged at moments into something like panic. When I have seen Harry it will be better. Or worse.

His bed was at the very end of the ward. There was noise that verged on pandemonium. Other visitors talked and shouted and two women were wailing, rocking to and fro, tears pouring down their faces. A porter clattered plates on a trolley. From beyond the open window motor-scooters buzzed constantly to and fro.

Harry was half-naked, his leg bundled like a cocoon, stripes of sticking-plaster all over him, a wodge of dressing on one shoulder. She sat beside him on a rickety chair and said, "This place is impossible. We'll have to get you out of here."

"It's O.K. People came this morning and took pictures for Italian telly. That bloke over there was in it too, and the old man at the end. And there's some women in another ward."

"Does your leg hurt?"

"Not all that much now. There are priests round every hour or so – never a dull moment."

"I'm going to talk to the doctor. See if we can't get you home."

The voices seemed to rise to a crescendo. Frances thought wildly, he can't stand this, I know I couldn't. Harry, suddenly, grinned. "Well, see Venice and die."

"Naples," said Frances. "Not Venice." And then, "*Must* you . . ."

She began to cry, copiously and unstoppably. Her face gave way; she found a wad of kleenex in her bag and dripped into it. Harry, scarlet with embarrassment, turned his head aside and froze.

"Sorry," she sniffed. She wiped the kleenex angrily across her eyes. "Though why it should be perfectly all right for Italian women to be weeping all over the place in public but not me I don't know."

He looked at her, cautiously.

"All right, I've finished. You can stop disowning me. Zoe sent her love. And Tab. You got your name in the papers, at home, you'll be interested to hear."

"Fame at last," said Harry.

He was sunburnt, and thin. His hair needed washing and lay against the pillow in black spikes. The first time she laid eyes on him she had been startled by his hair: she hadn't realised a baby could have so much. Black quills on that tiny skull, and the downy dent in the back of his neck.

"What do you need?"

Harry considered. "Things to read. Writing paper and a pen. Oh – and clothes. I've lost all my gear, or at least apparently it was pretty messed up."

She said at last, "Was it ghastly?"

Harry blinked. There came across his face the shuttered look of someone caught in a moment of privacy. He looked, for an instant, like a child. He said, "Actually it was shit, but I don't remember all that much. Just people screaming, and smoke everywhere. When you get the clothes, could you get some of those striped T-shirts like everyone wears here." A bell clanged. "They chuck you out now, it's the end of visiting-time."

"I'll see you tomorrow."

Dusk was falling when she got back to the hotel. It was on the waterfront, along from the Doge's Palace, in a different part of Venice to that in which she and Steven had stayed, which she could no longer place. It existed now for her only as a room with blowing white curtains and the sound of slapping water, and the chiming of a church clock.

She was very tired; everything seemed quite unreal. In the hospital, relief at seeing Harry and the realisation that he was at least relatively all right had given her a temporary lift. Now, that feeling of instability returned; walking into the foyer she felt quite dizzy and had to stand for a moment holding on to the reception desk while she waited for her key. Upstairs, she lay down for a while; she could not sleep and such bleakness descended upon her that she got up in a kind of panic and decided to go out and have a meal.

It was now quite dark. The Riva degli Schiavoni was awash with people. Brilliant ribbons of light quivered across the water. The air was still balmy and the stone of the bridge was warm to the touch. Everyone seemed to be laughing.

She sat down at the café outside the hotel and ordered a drink. At the next table, she saw suddenly, was the American woman who had been in the launch from the airport. She looked away quickly, avoiding her eye. The boy came with the drink and she fumbled with a fistful of lire, trying to find the right amount. And as she did so that dizziness returned, more forcefully; the lights swung and the pavement tipped and in slow motion she began to slide sideways. She heard the scrape of a chair and felt an arm round her. A voice said, "O.K., dear, just put your head down between your legs. That's it. You'll be all right in a moment." She hung, foolishly, over the pavement, and the tunnel down which she had been retreating faded and the arm held her down. The voice said, "Better? Try sitting up now. O.K.? Great."

Frances said weakly, "Thanks. Thanks so much. So stupid . . . I . . ."

"I guess you've got one of these stomach bugs," said the woman. "A week in Europe and sure as anything I have the runs. You are English, aren't you?"

"Yes. I don't think it is that. I only arrived this morning. I'm rather exhausted, that's all."

The waiter was still hanging around. The woman picked up Frances's bill, whisked a couple of notes from a purse. "*Grazie*."

"Oh no, you mustn't . . ."

"My pleasure. You're staying at this hotel too, I guess – I saw you get into the elevator. I just love all that gilt everywhere – you'd think they'd been around with a spray-gun. My shower has some kind of a jinx on it but apart from that the room seems O.K. How long are you staying? I'm Ruth Bowers, by the way."

"My name's Frances Brooklyn. I'm not too sure at the moment – probably a week or so." She drank her Cinzano and felt firmer. The faintness had gone; it was better, suddenly, to be with someone than alone. Ruth Bowers had crisp grey bangs and wore a different pair of metallic-framed uptilted glasses and another crisply laundered trouser-suit. She was the kind of person from whom Steven, by now, would have quietly retreated. She was talking about the friend with whom she was travelling and who had gone off to Yugoslavia for a few days and would meet up with Ruth in Rome. "We agreed from the start to go our own ways from time to time. I can't get enough of Italian painting and Ellen's – well, she can have too much of it. So she's giving the Tintorettos a miss and doing a hop to Zagreb. We're both librarians. Baltimore. Have you visited the United States, Frances?"

"I went there a couple of times with my husband. But not to Baltimore, I'm afraid." Frances felt pallid beside this woman's bristling energy. She must be at least sixty and exuded the physical charge of an electric toy, as though it were impossible she should ever run down.

"Well, it's quite a country! If you're ever there, stop by and visit – I'll give you the address. We're vacationing, of course – first time we were over since nineteen seventy-five and we see changes, I can tell you. We just love France, and last week when we were in Chartres, believe me there were . . ."

Ruth Bowers laid her hand, as she spoke, on Frances's arm and the physical contact was like a burn, distracting her totally. Two days after Steven's death she had lain in bed and thought, I shall never again feel someone else's arms round me, another person's body close up against mine, not sex, not nakedness, just physical closeness, often, casually, with another human being. And now the touch of others – Zoe's quick hugs, Tabitha's dutiful brushing of the cheek – had this disproportionate effect. To be touched was both a sacrilege and a joy.

" . . . But I guess nothing stands still and you've got to accept that. Now your country I just love. We had two weeks in London in seventy-five." The hand, the friendly emphasising hand, had been removed and Frances, picking herself up, said, "I live in London."

"Is that so? Is your husband joining you on vacation?"

Frances looked out at the glittering rivers of light, the myriads of strangers, at the permanent impervious skyline of dome and spire. "No. He died eight months ago. And I'm not on vacation, I'm here because my son is in hospital here. He was hurt in the airport explosion."

Ruth Bowers gave a kind of hiss. For a few moments she said nothing. Then, "Well, I guess you must think me really stupid, going on about vacations. One thing you can be sure of in this life, nothing's ever the way you think it is. I saw you on the boat, and back there in the hotel and I just had this impression of someone – well someone the sun shone on, if you see what I mean. You get to looking at people, when you're on your own. It's kind of nosy, I guess, but not all that much. I'm really sorry, Frances. How is your son?"

"He's not very badly hurt. A broken leg, and some cuts."

"That's really rough, though, having a kid caught up in something like that. You must've been worried sick. I don't have any kids myself – not married, for that matter – and I often think I missed something there. Someone you carried around inside your body – it grabs me just to think about it. Is he the only one?"

An oil tanker was passing between the quay and the distant skyline of Giudecca. Frances watched its huge grey bulk blot out the dome of San Giorgio. "As a matter of fact he isn't my son. He's adopted. There's a girl, too, a bit older. She was adopted too."

Ruth Bowers sighed. She gestured at the waiter. "If you'll excuse me, Frances, I'm going to buy us a couple more drinks. Oh my, this sure is my night for getting things wrong. But it's the same, I guess, isn't it, if you've had them from babies?"

"Oh yes," said Frances. "It's the same." She tried to find her purse. "Look, please let me . . ."

"Another time. You sit tight. You still look a bit rocky. You'd think they'd keep those darn great things out of the lagoon, wouldn't you? I read somewhere each of them carries enough crude oil to pollute twenty miles of coast-line. And from everything you hear this city's in enough trouble as it is. Did you see this booklet they have in the hotel about how they're appealing for . . ."

The tanker's silent passage extinguished the lights of the distant shore in sections, printing its shape upon the bright night. People passed and re-passed: singly, in groups, loitering, hurrying. It seemed amazing that there could be so many people, that the supply was endless, replenished every day, year in year out. The paving was worn smooth by feet, the joins between the stones almost obliterated. Probably, Frances thought, I walked along here with Steven, though I don't now remember. Maybe I have sat before in this exact spot, looking at the same skyline. Places are receptacles, that's all; they give nothing away, they don't record, they don't tell. They exist only in the head. In my head, this place is a white blown curtain, and water-noises, and Steven's voice, and my feelings. And now I see that there is more; all this was there then.

And with this knowledge there came a curious feverish resolve. I will learn this city, she thought, in the time that I am not with Harry at the hospital I will learn it, street by street. I will find in it that other time, those other days with Steven. It is all here, hitched to walls and paintings and the things we saw and smelled and heard, and I can get it back. I can have it again, hour by hour, and I don't care how much it hurts. I can reach out and take it back, and him with it.

"Hey, I've lost you, haven't I? Excuse me, I always talk too much. How are you feeling?"

"I'm sorry," Frances said. "I was in a daze, I'm afraid. But I do feel better now, thank you."

"Will you look at the time – nearly nine! My stomach's telling me that, too. I guess I'll go find somewhere to eat." Ruth Bowers hesitated. "I don't want to impose, but I think you could do with a meal too, Frances. Would you care to join me?"

"Thank you. I'd like to."

I have been here. I have seen this painting before. If I look hard enough, if I shut out now – these people, the noise, myself – I can bring back then. I remember the smell of this room, and the way the paintings have that hard bright glow. Steven said . . . Steven said something about looking at these huge pictures from the centre outwards . . . What did he say?

She stood in a crowd, in this hot room, and stared into the swirling tumultuous Annunciations and Resurrections and Calvaries and Ecce Homos. People weeping and people dying and people exulting and people praying; all those limbs and faces and shining flesh and flying garments; frame upon frame of it, gleaming like jewels in dark water, hanging there immutable before the crowds that come and melt away and come again with each new morning. For four hundred years eyes have stared at these paintings.

She sat on one of the benches at the side of the room. At this distance, the huge Annunciation became abstract, a swirling oval of light concentrating to a single central point. And the crowds ceaselessly shuffled before it, like the patient lines passing the coffin of some national hero, their heads turned for the allotted portion of time.

I don't remember all these people, back then. Were we quite alone here? Was Venice displayed just for us? Once, in a café, a man at the next table asked for the time; he spoke English, but was not English, and wore a fawn suit. In the hotel there was a French couple with children who ran about in the restaurant, knocking things over. So there were people.

What did Steven say, in here, looking at this picture? Think. Look long enough, and it will come back.

It does not come back. What comes, instead, is one of the confusing intrusive wisdoms of hindsight. The cloak of Christ, in that Agony in the Garden, is a rich ruby red and the colour, devoured by an eye that sees but does not observe, recreates another such wine-dark velvety splash, the wing of one of the chairs in the Putney house – a wing against which rests Steven's head, bent down over papers on his lap. He looks up, and the papers rustle under his hands. He says, "You've been crying." He shuffles the papers together. He says, "You must have children, darling, because if you don't you will go quietly nuts. So something has got to be done."

She went out into the piazza. She passed from the shadow of an arcade into the sun and the heat stunned her. She stood looking around and for an instant, a worrying instant, could not think where she was, why she was there. She could have been dreaming; the buildings, the colonnades, the dome of a church, were like the fantasy landscape of a dream. The moment fled, and she knew again. That morning she had seen Harry, and he was more or less out of pain, and the doctor had said he might be able to walk with crutches in a week, but could not be moved until then. She was in Venice, and it was mid-afternoon, and she had in her hand a map and a guide-book.

She moved into the shade and looked at the map. She opened the guide-book, and read. Names on the pages quivered and set up answering vibrations in her mind. Did we not go there? Don't I remember that? Carpaccio, Donatello, Verrocchio, San Stefano, San Rocco, Santa Maria della Salute. She stared at the map, and the geometry of the streets and squares reeled and shimmered. She set off, across open spaces and down alleyways and over bridges. The city ensnared her like a web, a maze. When she tried to match her position to the lines and names on the map there seemed to be no possible relationship. What was, and what was said to be, were not the same. The crumbling fading landscape of arches and pillars and snatches of water and curving bridges and ever-shifting skylines was a stage-set, a tricksy deceptive palimpsest. Alleys furtively opened in walls that appeared blank; streets swung round corners into concealed squares; canals blocked her passage. She abandoned the map and simply wandered, digested by the city. She saw nothing that related in any way to that other time. Once, a statue halted her, setting up some reverberation, but when she looked harder she realised that it resembled a bronze of a horse and rider in a London street.

She went into a church. At the entrance, a placard announced its date and listed its treasures. Inside, she sat for a moment on a chair, in the scented gloom; footsteps tapped and whispered on the marble floor. She got up and wandered from painting to painting; Madonnas and Christs and the patriarchal cloaked figures of biblical mythology. Each picture was a complex system of reference and meaning; it told a story. It assumed in the viewer an answering set of responses. If you did not know the language of Christianity these paintings would be meaningless; works of art, no more and no less. She found her own knowledge wanting from time to time. Who was Emmaus? The Maccabees? Saint Barbara? Above all, the tableaux, the faces, the emotions seemed to exist outside the straitjacket of time, to be as permanent and detached as natural landscape. Their power was aesthetic, the frozen grief or rejoicing upon the faces was as safely beyond actual sorrow or joy as were the bearers of those names on the tombstones in that London burial ground.

She stood before a triptych Virgin and Child and felt more utterly alone than at any point since Steven's death.

Chapter Five

On the morning of the third day Frances tried to telephone Zoe. She had already done so once but, finding her out, had left a message on the answering machine. Now she again fumbled with the unfamiliar mechanism of an Italian phone-box. She dialled the international code and distant voices chattered at her. She had no idea where in the city she was; she had lost the map and discarded the guide-book. When at last Zoe's distorted recorded voice replied she left another message.

It must be the third day because of the date on the newspaper she had taken to Harry that morning. Otherwise, the time since she had been here had merged into a continuous present, exempt from the conventional divisions of day and night, eating and sleeping. She had returned to the hotel when she was too exhausted to go on wandering the city, slept and eaten when it occurred to her. The only fixed points had been her twice daily visits to Harry. She had sat by his bed for the prescribed time, had talked to him, had brought him the things he needed. He was something of a celebrity in the hospital, petted by the nurses and visited by the relatives of other inmates of the ward, who gathered around his bed smiling and pressing on him small gifts by way of chocolate, fruit and even flowers. An ambulant patient was teaching him Italian. He sat by Harry's bed, patiently enunciating, a huge amiable man stripped to a pair of pyjama trousers above which rose a torso blanketed with curly black hair. When Frances arrived he would rise, bowing and grinning, and pad away again to his own bed.

"You're all right here, then?"

"It's O.K. The doctor says I'll have another X-ray tomorrow and then they'll know when I can go."

"Yes. I've seen him too. He thinks possibly at the weekend. I'm going to book flights in case."

She talked to him mechanically, hardly knowing what she said, hearing her own voice as though it were someone else's. From time to time she would see him suddenly, with a sharper awareness, and was astonished by him: his lanky adult body, his man's voice, his laconic remarks. Once, she said, "Do you remember that time you got stuck on a cliff in Cornwall?" Harry stared for a moment, blankly: "Oh God – yes, vaguely. I'd had a fight with Tab. It was a bit of machismo stuff. How old was I?" "About ten." "I remember thinking Dad would give me a roasting but all he said was, 'That was a pointless thing to do, as you presumably now realise.' Dad never went in for recriminations, did he?" "No, he didn't."

Harry frowned. He lay staring at the ceiling and then flashed her a sideways look in which lurked embarrassment, compunction and loss of words. He said, "Don't feel you need hang around here, Mum. I mean, why don't you have a look at Venice while you're at it." He turned away again and his black hair which, now, someone had washed, lay in strands upon the pillow.

As thus, then, it stands in quills against the electric blue nylon blanket in which he lies swathed in a plastic carry-cot in the office of the adoption society to which they have driven, almost in silence, through south London. Relax, said Steven, once, putting out a hand, laying it for a moment on her knee, relax for goodness sake. You're as stiff as a poker, I can feel it. You're going to fetch a baby, not stand trial for murder. And she looks down into the carry-cot where this infant, this alien infant, is fast asleep, snuffling gently like an asthmatic dog. She looks at the dark quills and, when suddenly he turns his head, the soft dent in the back of his neck invokes in her a sensation of internal dissolution not unlike sexual desire. She wants to pick him up and clamp him to her breast. She knows that she does not give a damn whose he is or where he comes from. She stares down at him and behind her Steven and the adoption society lady are talking and she does not hear a word they say.

"Actually," she said, "I've been here before. Dad and I spent our honeymoon here. Surely we must have talked about it . . ." And Harry, embarrassed again, replies that oh yes, sure, he'd forgotten, but anyway . . . I suppose I'll never get to see the Doge's Palace and all that now, he went on, the whole point of coming here . . .

"You've got all your life," said Frances. "Venice will continue."

The process of transition from one place to another was as

mechanical as her conversations with Harry. She was in the hospital, and then somehow she was back in the city, walking, sitting at a café, passing through arcades from flaring light to deep shadow. She went in and out of the hotel, waited for the lift, locked and unlocked the door of her room.

On one of these visits she was aware of the American woman, Ruth Bowers, beside her. "I'm sorry?"

"I just wondered if you'd care to meet up for a meal later."

"Oh," said Frances, confused. "How nice – yes, well, maybe." She stared round the hotel lobby. In locked display cases were examples of Venetian glass: tormented structures of extreme ugliness – animals, fluted vases, encrusted bowls. She saw them with great intensity – their boiled sweet colours, the twists and pleats and bubbles of the glass. Like the rest of the physical world, they had the sharpness of accessories in dreams; she was acutely aware of sight and sound. The world seemed to glow and roar around her. "For lunch, you mean?"

"Frances," said Ruth Bowers. "It's past four o'clock in the afternoon now. Look, dear, I don't want to pry, but are you sure you're all right at the moment. I passed you in the piazza this morning and you seemed kind of dazed."

"I'm fine," said Frances. "Truly." She achieved, from somewhere, a smile, a brisk reassuring smile. "Enjoying the sights. Harry's getting on well, they say. Do let's meet up tomorrow." And smiling still she left Ruth Bowers, who watched her go, seeing a woman with unkempt hair, dark pouches under her eyes and a crumpled skirt.

At some point that evening, when Frances was sitting at a café in one of the smaller and more hidden squares, she knew that she had been here before, on this precise spot. She looked up at the floodlit façade of a church and knew that that same arrangement of pink and apricot light was lodged within her head, the accompaniment to Steven's voice asking if she would like to go to a concert. She is wearing a pink striped dress; they have eaten a delicious meal; from time to time, with tranquil pleasure, she wonders if she is pregnant. She looks up at this glowing floating church and Steven asks if she would like to go to a concert. And the whiff of all this hung still in the square as she had known it would if only she searched long enough. The public place became private, hers alone, and she sat there until the peace that she had won tipped suddenly back into restless uncertainty. The waiter, his eye on the solitary woman who had sat so long with a single drink, saw her rise in sudden agitation and watched her hurry away, one drab foreign tourist among many.

She telephoned, and again Zoe was not there. She left a message, a bleak sentence delivered with painful urgency: "What colour were Steven's eyes?"

On the morning of the fourth day Ruth Bowers began to follow Frances through the streets of Venice. She trotted some twenty or thirty paces behind, weaving deftly through the crowds, and at the points when she thought Frances might turn and see her she would stop to stare in a shop window, or study the details of a building. In fact, these ruses were quite unnecessary, as she suspected: Frances was seeing nothing.

In London, Zoe, returning to her flat, pressed the switch of her answering machine before pouring two glasses of whisky, one for herself and one for Eric Sadler. When Frances's voice came through, first once and then – after another message from someone else – again, Zoe put down her glass and stood staring at the machine. She listened once more to the messages. She said, "I knew I should have gone with her."

She looked at Eric and said, "I have this blasted assignment in Edinburgh tomorrow", and Eric, a big man with grizzled hair and the sagging belly of the desk-bound scowled for a moment in thought and then said, "Hang on, lovey, didn't you say that pal of yours – what's-his-name, the musical guy – didn't you say he was in Venice?"

"Morris!" cried Zoe, "You clever sod. Dead right – he was going there to lecture to something or other."

There was something she should do, but she could not think what it was. Some obligation that tugged like the reality lying beyond the compulsive world of a dream. She walked out into the morning knowing that there was some person she should visit, with whom she was concerned. Standing in the drumming heat of the piazza she knew suddenly that it was Harry, that she was here in Venice with Harry, but she no longer remembered why, or where he might be. She was in a condition of juddering nervousness. The calm grey state of grief had gone and in its place had come a jagged anxiety bordering on panic; her legs felt weak and she found herself constantly holding on to things – balustrades, the backs of chairs – as though she were physically infirm and might fall. She walked through streets and squares and saw nothing: the houses and churches and canals rolled by like stage-sets. She was obsessed, isolated, locked within herself, in feverish pursuit. She knew that something disastrous was happening to her, that possibly she was going mad, and she knew also that if she ceased for one moment to think about Steven, to carry him with her in her head, she might lose him. He was dead; he existed only in recollection; when recollection ceased even that tenuous existence would be gone. A name, no more. Like the host of names on the white tombstones of Bunhill Fields burial ground; the silent army beneath the soil.

She brought back his face, his touch, his voice. She listened to the things he said, significant or trivial. The past lost all chronology; its jumbled fragments came and went with kaleidoscopic brilliance. She wandered into a church and stood before pictures that she did not see. Turning to leave she was vaguely aware of a woman who made as though to speak to her, a woman with grey curls and tilt-framed sun-glasses. She smiled at the woman, whom she recognised as an acquaintance, and went quickly past her and out into the street; she could no longer afford intrusions or interruptions.

She was alone now with Steven; the survival of his memory rested with her. She no longer had, herself, any sense of time; she did not know how long she had been in Venice any more than she could remember quite why she had come except, she now began to believe, in search of Steven. He was here, as he was also in London and Cambridge and on a lawn in Sussex and on a hillside in Dorset; she could visit him in these places, and to be with him thus would save him from the awful oblivion beyond memory. I loved you so much, she said to him, and you were always stronger than I am, you knew what had to be done and how to do it, you did not need me as I needed you, but now there is something that I can do for you that you cannot do for yourself, and only I can do it.

She leaned on the parapet of a canal bridge and saw a dead cat float past, a bundle of clotted fur. She heard church bells and the laughter of two young men. Somewhere, a caged bird sang. Sweat trickled down her spine; she had been walking now for two or three hours. She continued to ransack her memory and there came an image of Steven entering the London house, dropping his briefcase beside the little marble-topped table, wiping rain from his spectacles with a red handkerchief, and this was almost at once replaced by another in which he lay beside her in bed, reading, cold-faced and shut off into that world of his own concerns, and another in which he spoke from a television screen, disembodied against a nile-green background. Clenched in the passenger seat of the Ford, she travelled with him down a French road, the kilometres ticking away to the swish-swish of the poplars, another hour-and-a-half, another forty minutes . . . "Take it easy, Frances," he says. "Nearly there now," and his hand lies on her knee. And presently they stand above the bed in which lies Zoe, looking pale, depleted. "Give us a kiss," says Zoe. "Tell me how clever I am." And with a twitch of whatever uncontrollable mechanism decides these things that picture was replaced by another of Steven on the far side of the kitchen, hostile and sarcastic, but the words of the quarrel had gone, try as she might to resurrect them. That was not happiness, perfect or imperfect, but must be retrieved and kept along with other things; life is whole and undivided.

She looked along the canal and saw the cat caught in a scum of refuse by a flight of steps. A vaporetto chugged past, its varnished wood flashing in the sunlight. She no longer had that sense of panic; instead there had come a kind of dull confusion. Someone, she knew, expected her. There was someone she had to visit, to find. Zoe? No, not Zoe. She went back over the bridge and down a small alley that led to a square in which was a statue of a horse and rider. And, as she walked past this, seeing the brilliant green streaks on the metal and the graffiti incised on the rump of the horse she felt once more that assurance of having been here before, both welcome and disturbing. But the familiarity was different. It was not, this time, a sense of then but of now. It was not that she was revisiting this particular spot, but that this was where she ought to be, the point for which she had been searching, for days or for hours – she no longer knew which.

A square. A statue. A church. And over there a street that would lead to another on which was the hotel. A small, moderately-priced hotel with a red and white striped awning over the entrance and petunias in pots on the window-ledges.

The panic was quite gone now. She knew where she was. And she was happy, perfectly happy. The sun had sunk and the afternoon had entered that phase of steamy heat before the evening; she felt that she must be late, and hurried the last few yards to the end of the street. There round the corner was the hotel and seeing it she felt a further lift of the spirits. It seemed silly, now, to have been searching for so long. It was stupid to have lost the map. She must get there quickly and explain. She must have been gone for ages. She ran up the steps and into the entrance hall.

When Ruth Bowers came into the hotel Frances was standing at the reception desk. She was asking for her key. The perplexity of the porter and Frances's urgency filled the small space with tension. The porter kept shaking his head and Frances kept on asking. "I'm sorry," she kept saying, "I just don't remember the number, but it's on the second floor." Ruth laid a hand on her arm and Frances turned. In her eyes there was confused recognition. "Oh, hello again," she said. "It's so silly – I got myself completely lost. I simply couldn't find this place. My husband must have been waiting ages."

Ruth Bowers moved her hand to her elbow and began to steer her away. "Don't worry about that just now, dear. We can sort all that out later." And as she led Frances out into the street Frances stared at her and said, "I'm not sure where I am." "I know, dear," said Ruth Bowers, "I know. Just don't worry about it."

The curtains that blew in the light breeze from the open window were not white but flowered, a riotous arrangement of poppies and tendrilled things like passion flowers. Frances, waking from long deep sleep, lay looking at them. Presently, turning her head, she saw an envelope on the carpet by the door. She got up, opened it, and read a note from Ruth Bowers in which Ruth hoped that she had slept well and felt better; "That doctor certainly carried some kind of super knock-out pill – you were out cold before I tucked you up last night. I'm off for a final look at Santa Maria – my friend joins me tomorrow – and I'll drop back later in the morning to see how you're going on."

It was ten o'clock. She rang down for some coffee, and dressed. She felt heavy, a little dopey still, but otherwise quite normal. At eleven she could go to the hospital to visit Harry. When the coffee came she sat by the window drinking it, and read Ruth's note again. And as she did so she was filled with emotion. Tears sprang to her eyes. Why should the kindness of strangers be so unnerving? She put the note back in its envelope and went to the dressing-table. From the mirror, a pale face looked at her with tired, anxious eyes. She began to comb her hair and then with sudden revulsion went into the bathroom and washed it, using soap in the absence of any shampoo. Then she sat in the sun on the little balcony beyond the window and let it dry on her shoulders. When she went back to the mirror it had dried to a coarse bounciness that reminded her of the effect of boarding-school shampooings with institutional soap-mix provided in huge vats, when she was a girl. Thus, time was, she had tugged combs through the same hair, fringing the same face, the head tumultuous with quite other preoccupations. Except, of course, that the hair was not the same at all – had grown since then by goodness how many yards, been discarded goodness how many times, was flecked now in one spot with a thin line of grey. And the face had undergone phase upon phase of change so that, looking at it, she saw, or pictured, like a flickering film, each remembered version right back to that fifteen-year-old schoolgirl, and acknowledged with a kind of sad indulgence this tribe of alter egos; innocents – unknowing unsuspecting innocents.

She checked the contents of her handbag, locked her door and went down in the lift. When she stepped out into the foyer she noticed at the reception desk a man she had seen somewhere before: a short man with greying bristly hair and a small pointed beard. And as she tried to remember who he was he turned, saw her, looked at once relieved and embarrassed and said, "Mrs Brooklyn – I don't know if you remember . . . We met for a few moments in Cambridge, with Zoe. Morris Corfield."

"Yes. Of course. What a funny coincidence – you're staying here too?"

"Well, no. Elsewhere, in fact. I'm in Venice to give some

lectures to a summer school. I just looked in to see if there was anything I could do to help. Zoe said you were here. How is your son?"

"Getting on well, thank you. I hope I'll be told soon when I can take him home." Why did the man look so uncomfortable?

"Zoe," he went on after a moment, "was a bit concerned. She wondered if you . . . There was a phone message you'd left . . ."

He had brown eyes, of a noticeable intense colour almost as dark as the pupil: disposition, if it shows at all, shows in the eyes. These were unassuming, faintly melancholy, and, at the moment, embarrassed. "A phone message? I haven't rung Zoe."

"Oh," he said, "In that case . . . Well, some muddle, I expect – but anyway she just felt a bit worried and asked me to look in if I was this way and see if you needed anything. The heat," he continued with a rush, "rather gets one down. Like a sauna, I always think, Venice at this time of year. I shan't be sorry to get back to London." He looked at her, enquiring. Meaning well.

And Frances, gazing beyond him, over his shoulder out to the teeming pavement, blinked and said at last, "It's quite possible I did ring Zoe. As a matter of fact I don't remember anything at all that happened yesterday. Or much of the last few days. An American woman who is staying here seems very kindly to have coped last night." She paused. "I feel . . . rather foolish."

Morris Corfield said, "Why don't we have some coffee?"

Hours later, in the evening, she sat opposite him in a restaurant. He had told her that he was here to lecture on Baroque music to American girls at a summer school – "Disconcertingly large sums of money for a rather low level of address" – that he was music critic for a weekly paper and was writing a book on

Scarlatti. He had talked of his son and mentioned that his wife left him a number of years ago. He had spoken affectionately of Zoe. They had discussed the problems of getting Harry back to England with his leg in plaster. Now, he looked at her across the scraped plates and the half-empty wine-glasses and asked delicately, "Are you feeling more . . . more yourself now?"

"Yes, thank you." She drank some coffee. She put down the cup and studied the circle of dregs. "I seem to have had some sort of crisis in which for a while I didn't really know what was going on. This person – Ruth Bowers – apparently found me in the hotel where I spent my honeymoon. I seemed to think that Steven was there."

There was a small silence. "Stupid," she said.

"Not at all. Entirely understandable. You must have been under a great strain, this last couple of weeks."

"I had thought," Frances went on bleakly, "that I was beginning to get a little better. I'm sorry to talk as though I were an invalid, but bereavement is in a way like chronic illness."

Morris Corfield said, "So I understand. But you're . . . all right today?"

"Much better. A little muzzy still. A doctor gave me some sleeping pills. But I know the difference between then and now." She smiled, with an effort.

"It's obviously unfortunate you had to come here, when it has these associations."

"Everywhere has associations, in some way or another. But yes, Venice seems to have unhinged me, a little. I'm sorry – let's stop talking about my problems."

"Only if you wish to," said Morris.

She looked at him. All right, she thought, it's probably good for me to talk, even at the risk of boring this poor kind man. All the better that it should be someone I shall in all probability never set eyes on again.

"I have had this nightmarish feeling that if I don't clutch on to everything I remember of Steven he will disappear completely. That I am responsible for him and that if I forget anything his memory will be cancelled entirely. Here, it has seemed to take me over – I've been unable to think of anything else."

"But it isn't only you who remembers him. Lots of people do. In that way he survives many times over."

"I know. Rationally I know that. Emotionally I don't. Anyway," Frances went on, (thinking, you don't understand – no one can who has not been submerged in this . . .) "it isn't really anything to do with other people. It is private."

"Yes. I see that."

"I have always expected too much," she said rapidly. "I have always planned too much. I've always lived ahead rather than backwards. When Steven died I stopped dead. Being unhappy is an occupation – you hardly notice anything else."

He nodded.

"I expected marriage to be other than it turned out. I expected to have children and never did. I expected Steven to be immortal. And now suddenly the past seems to me as unreliable as the future."

"How?" said Morris Corfield, warily.

"Nothing is as you thought it was. Everything is changed by all that comes after."

"Oh yes. I've noticed that too."

"I keep remembering happiness as though it were some

foreign language that I once knew and have forgotten. I don't seem to know any more what it was like."

"Come," he said gently. "You can't have been happy all the time. No one is."

"I don't mean contentment or comfort or companionship. I mean absolute happiness. Those times when . . ." she looked away, ". . . when how you feel seems to fuse with the physical world. That sounds fey. It seems the only way to put it."

"No. I understand. I remember first experiencing it as a small boy. Something to do with snow falling and the sight of it heaped on a branch and elation over Christmas presents. Very self-sufficient, children. It's only later that such times become centred on other people."

There was a pause. The restaurant was emptying. Outside, the Venetian evening smouldered.

Frances said, "And I have these fears that perhaps even such moments were not so at all. Since now there is only me to think of them. As though I didn't share them with Steven at all."

She was filled, as she spoke, with a sense of betrayal. To talk of Steven like this to a stranger; Steven, that most private of men. Forgive me, she thought, but this is what I have come to.

Morris Corfield said, "It is of course pointless to say don't do so much thinking. You are obliged to."

"I'm afraid so."

"Nor is it easy to offer any consolation that isn't just . . . superficial. I remember feeling somewhat the same when my wife left me. What she did seemed to change the time we had together. But your husband didn't leave you. Dying is different."

"I know," said Frances wearily. She wished, suddenly, that

she had never got into this. She wanted to go back to the hotel, and to bed.

Morris lit a small cigar. "As for happiness . . . Isn't it more often a personal experience anyway? Is it something shared? My feeling is that it happens to one in isolation."

"But because of someone else, usually."

"I suppose so." He flapped at the cigar smoke in sudden concern. "I'm sorry – do you mind this thing?"

"Not at all."

"If I may say so, you seem to have suffered from a curious mixture of idealism and romanticism. So much expectation."

"Oh," said Frances. "Aren't most people like that?"

"I doubt it. Evidently your husband wasn't from what you say. Or rather from what you have not said."

"He wasn't much like me, no."

"And the children are adopted?"

"Yes."

"They know?"

"Of course. Not . . . all the details."

Morris sat frowning at the tablecloth. At last he said, "It's difficult for someone who has never gone through what you have to know what to say. I imagine that one of the many . . . difficulties . . . is this question of adjusting to . . . no, assimilating . . . all the things you remember. I hope it will get easier. I'm sure it will. You seem to me a very . . . well, a very stable sort of person."

There was a silence. They both shifted in their chairs, suddenly uneasy. Frances began to wonder how to insist on paying her share of the bill, which lay at Morris's elbow. Snatch it up, as Zoe would? Slip across the appropriate notes?

Morris put out his cigar, frowning then at the stub as though it offended him. "Is there anything I can do in a practical sense? Book you a flight – that kind of thing?"

"Thank you," said Frances. "It's very kind, but I've seen to all that. We go the day after tomorrow."

"Ah. Well, I'm sure back in London everything will seem . . . not quite so bad." The sentence trailed away. Frances, grimly accustomed to the responses of embarrassment and faint panic that her condition generated in others thought: poor man, plunged into all this. She began to talk brightly of the new house to which she was moving. Morris picked up the bill.

"Please let me . . ." she dived for her purse.

"Certainly not. All these ill-gotten dollars I have . . . Waiter!"

They walked through the night-time city, in which the floodlit buildings glowed like stage-sets, doubly unreal, detached both from time and place. Domes and façades hung in the darkness, wonderful survivors, speaking of mysteries. And before them flowed that river of people, strolling, hurrying, talking, renewing itself every hour and every day. Men and women and children. Morris and Frances, side by side, a little awkward with one another, concerned with the formalities of parting. Stopping at last on the corner by the Doge's Palace, shaking hands, thanking and hesitating and walking away at last separately into the gilded evening.

Chapter Six

"You shouldn't have done it," said Ruth Bowers. "Those flowers. They must've cost an arm and a leg. But I love them. I don't know when I last got given flowers." She laughed. "They don't often come my way."

Frances said, "You've been so kind. You really have. What I don't understand is how you happened to be there – at the other hotel."

"Now this is where you're maybe going to get angry with me, Frances, but I followed you. I could see when you went out in the morning there was something wrong. So I thought well, better maybe to play it safe and I just hung around with you for a while. Well, for most of the day. We looked at a lot of pictures, remember?"

"I don't see how I could be angry. It was extraordinarily good of you. I don't remember the pictures at all."

"Donatello. Carpaccio. You name it . . . We did a real hard

day. But I didn't think at the time you were taking much in. And then you dashed off down this street as though something had come into your head all of a sudden and I thought, hey, this looks peculiar . . . And that was how it was."

"Do you think I'm ill?"

"No," said Ruth briskly, "I'd say you weren't. I think you just kind of collapsed briefly through being overtired and overstrained and generally het up. I'd say you were all better now. Maybe you should check up with your doctor when you get home, but I don't think you're ill."

She wore, this morning, yet another pastel trouser suit and a peaked cap pulled tightly down over her grey hair, the fringe sticking out below it. This is a good woman, Frances thought, you expect goodness to go around with some sort of distinguishing mark – uniforms and robes and discreet medals – but when it turns up it is decked with apricot crimplene and an ugly jockey cap and gilt-framed sun-glasses. Nothing is ever as it seems to be. She said, "After my husband – Steven – died I was determined to get through it all on my own. The doctor kept trying to give me some sort of tranquilliser but I wouldn't take them."

"Good for you. Stay that way."

"But this is a bit . . . well, a bit unnerving. Suppose it happens again?"

"Why should it? Listen, Frances, I guess some people would say you should see a shrink. And I'd say don't. I'm not very typical. Most of my friends have been in therapy at one time or another and you know what puzzles me about it? It's the idea that there's any kind of tidy answer to things. Life doesn't seem to me like that – it's a mess. But most people – or at least most people back home – go at it like they were after the secret of the universe. Just find the right formula and you'll get happy. You'll hit on the answer like you might hit on the right colour-scheme for the living-room and the sun will come out and shine for ever after. Coming to terms with life, that's what it's called. But personally I don't see how you come to terms with something that's basically fouled-up in a lot of ways. And I don't call that pessimism, I call it common sense. You know what I think? I think it's a misplaced faith in science. This is a scientific age and by heavens it ought to come up with a scientific answer to everything. Even how to get through life without trouble. Excuse me, Frances, I talk too much. How's your boy doing?"

"Very well, apparently. We can go home early tomorrow."

"I see they caught one of the guys that did it. But the guy was a girl."

"Yes."

"Twenty-one years old. Jesus! I mean, when I was twenty-one years old I was worrying about whether my lipstick was the right shade."

They sat on the terrace of a café, in the shade of a pergola. Morning glory flowers drooped and turned purple, their brief moment already gone. Pigeons milled around the tables. Frances, earlier, had worked out that she must have been in Venice for a week. She had telephoned Zoe and eventually reached her at her office. I'm all right, she had said, quite all right. I wasn't for a while but I am now, and I'm sorry I got you worried, it seems I left some stupid message. Blow that, said Zoe, forget it, skip it, just talk now I've got you. Did Morris Corfield look you up? He paid for your dinner. Good for him, then. And now when do we see you?

Ruth Bowers was leaving the next day to meet up with her friend in Rome. Frances said, "Could we keep in touch?"

"Sure we'll keep in touch. I'm the type that keeps in touch. I show up, uninvited." She grinned, with the glimmer of a gold-capped tooth.

Frances examined herself. She examined her state of mind and found it not too bad. She was not agitated any more, the sense of panic had gone, it was possible calmly to see to things like plane reservations and the cashing of travellers' cheques. She was trudging once more that level grey plain of sorrow. But there were one or two curiosities, to be inspected and considered. The flow of warmth she had felt for Ruth Bowers, a stranger, and the faint but inescapable satisfaction that she was alone in this encounter. Steven would not have cared for Ruth Bowers. Steven would have found Ruth Bowers tedious and ultimately uninteresting. Which she is not, Frances thought. Which I think she is not.

The second curiosity was the fact that she had seen this city, today and yesterday, for odd moments, as a place in its own right, independent and untouched by what went before. Accompanying Ruth on a last walk round the central area, she had found herself looking at the façade of a building with eyes that were shriven; she saw the windows and the pillars and the flaking pink stucco for themselves and not in any relationship to that other time. Whether she had passed this way then, with Steven, was neither here nor there; she wanted, simply to know the name of this particular palazzo and when it was built. She examined, now, this response and found it interesting.

Harry was out of bed and walking with crutches, egged on

with cries of encouragement by his fellow patients. Well-wishers came to see him in the ward and stood over his bed, uttering condolences in broken English or simply beaming. Harry, who at school had maintained a stubborn and unfashionably xenophobic refusal to attempt foreign languages, had acquired a good deal of inaccurate but valiant Italian. Watching him joke with the nurses Frances was astonished; she saw suddenly the man he would presently be, with attitudes and mannerisms all his own, derived beyond childhood, unfamiliar. He had been interviewed by journalists and television people; one of the articles was translated for her by the doctor, along with Harry's curiously laconic replies. The doctor, holding the newspaper from which stared Harry's passport photograph, three years younger in school uniform, said, "Your son is very . . . tolerant. He does not grudge. That people should do such a thing."

"I think he feels rather as I do. It seems more like some awful – Act of God – rather than something people have done."

"Act of God . . ." said the doctor. He grimaced, throwing the newspaper into a bin. "I have examined him this morning. He is well. The leg is going all right. There will be no scars. Only maybe" – he grimaced again – "inside."

Frances said, "Thank you for looking after him so well."

In fact, it seemed to her that Harry had taken it all very calmly. Apart from that one moment of candour – "It was shit" – he had not referred again to the time at the airport and had seemed mainly interested in all that had come after – the life of the hospital, the people he had met there, his own situation. For someone to whom, in a brief lifetime, nothing violent had ever happened before he appeared to be reassuringly stoical. He's doing better than I have, Frances thought. Within a year he has seen his father die and been blown up in a foreign country by people of whose existence he had never heard; perhaps, after this, he will grow up with expectations of a different kind from mine, and maybe that will be all the better for him.

Until she was eighteen nothing had ever happened to her. She had grown up wrapped in the bland self-deception of a mother who refused to contemplate misfortune. It was a mindlessly placid world in which things would always work out for the best, in which one must look on the bright side, in which dead pets had gone to sleep, the old were mercifully released and illness was just a matter of a few days in bed. Her mother's concerns were domestic and local, bounded by the school of which her husband was headmaster, the parents connected therewith, other people she knew and, at a stretch, matters of wider parochial interest such as structural alterations to the landscape of the small market town in which they lived. She never read newspapers and, as Frances presently realised, lived throughout the development of nuclear weapons and the advent of the Cold War without apparently having any idea of the implications of either. Years later, Frances sat out the Cuba crisis with a hard fist of fear in her stomach, the children playing at her feet during the pulsing signature theme of the news bulletins, a sound that would for ever afterwards induce queasiness. She stared at the faces of statesmen, at ships ploughing across a gleaming quilted sea. The world turned, uncontrollable. Her mother, telephoning one evening, talked of weather and the school prize-giving – "The news, darling? Oh, I know, I know – but these things always blow over, don't they?" The first time Frances brought Steven home he had become involved in an argument about politics with her father. Her mother had been shocked by his intensity: "I mean it's not as though it was something personal. Just the government, and that sort of thing. I don't understand people getting so heated. Of course, I can see he's very clever." She had not liked Steven, who in turn had treated her with the scrupulous politeness that conceals contempt. And who can blame him, thought Frances. They didn't breathe the same air.

When she was eighteen she had gone to university and discovered that life is insecure. She read, and the world expanded before her eyes. She saw possibilities, and learned the practice of expectation. She joined every organisation that offered itself, in a desperate bolt from the burrow in which she had grown up, and then became alarmed by what seemed to her the anonymity of public involvement, and threw away her Young Liberal card, her Debating Society card, her French Club card, her United Nations Group card . . . By the time she met Steven she had withdrawn into a different kind of privacy: not her mother's privacy of ignorance but another one. The privacy of resistance. She was affronted by the presumption that what happens to people is – has to be – conditioned from beyond. She wanted both to plan and to control her own life. Steven, though as opportunist as all ambitious men, would never have conceded the possibility of this. In fact, they never discussed it; Frances made plans and Steven noted the course of events and acted expediently. And when the devils grinned and the world shrugged and Frances's plans went astray, Steven made crisp recommendations. If Frances mourned what was lost, he told her with irritation how to retrieve what could be retrieved, how to side-step and change position. She listened, knowing that she could not change herself.

And now, in Venice, in another existence, she looked with surprise at Harry, sitting in a wicker chair on the balcony of the hospital, his plastered leg stuck out in front of him, asking her when they were moving to the new house. She had almost forgotten about the house that must be moved to, and the house that must be moved from.

"No," said Zoe. "No way. Yes. Tell them to get stuffed. Right. 'Bye." She put the phone down on the man in the Paris office and made three more calls, booking a flight to Dublin and cancelling two arrangements for the next couple of days. Blown all her working life by unpredictable demands, this did not disturb her at all. Conditioned, indeed, to expect the unexpected, she would have been more disconcerted by a week in which she had done precisely what her engagement diary told her she was likely to be doing. She made a further call to the secretary of the politician in Dublin who had – unexpectedly – agreed to be interviewed and set about packing an overnight bag.

As she did so, she thought of Frances. The overnight bag, as it happened, was a present from Frances; it catered, by way of many compartments and miraculously folding extensions, for the wayward traveller, rashly over-burdening herself. And Zoe, cramming things into it now, saw Frances, holding out the beribboned Christmas present, saying, I hope it's right, there were so many different kinds, and I'm such a non-travelling person myself . . . And Steven, indulgently allowing the superficialities of Christmas to wash over him. Harry, with his first electric razor. Tab, sparkling over the silver necklace one had pounced on in the market in Teheran, seeing it already around her neck. Objects. Possessions. The material world that we carry around with us, that solders us to events, that outlasts them. The objects with which we manifest love. The possessions with which we possess.

She dialled her office with a message for Frances should she call before her return from Dublin. Tell her I'm back tomorrow evening at latest. Tell her the estate agent rang and I've taken care of it. Tell her . . .

No, don't tell her I've been worried stiff about her.

I've known Frances all my adult life. For twenty-five years she has been there. Friendship is the love that is ignored; people don't theorise about friendship, write poetry about it. It just goes quietly along, sustaining. Passion spends itself – oh my goodness, does passion spend itself – but friendship is always there. Like a good marriage, it survives attack. I have loved – let me see – four men. Loved to the point of temporary derangement. And of all that spent emotion I remember not a thing. Those times of him-not-telephoning and him-not-being-there and jealousy and doubt are quite gone – oh, the sequence of events still vaguely lingers but the emotion is irretrievable. Like all extinguished pain. But the feeling for Frances is constant, permanent. Like love for children.

Lying in a bed, once upon a time somewhere in France, exhausted, ripped in half, looking up at Frances (her face . . . in which joy and worry contend . . .), saying, there, tell me how clever I am, she's gorgeous, take her, quick . . .

She made a further call to the office and left for Heathrow. On the plane she sat reading a file of clippings provided by the office. In Dublin, she sought various quarry, ending with a long smoke-laden session with the politician during which his evasions were matched by Zoe's guile, a process appreciated by both of them.

She went to her hotel and sat in her room for a couple of hours scowling and typing. At half-past ten she descended to the hotel bar and saw instantly on the far side of the red plush room in which musak softly seeped from the walls and American tourists sat plumply padded out with Arran sweaters one of those four men she once frenziedly loved. The man, a fellow journalist, looked up over his glass and waved. Zoe joined him.

"Well, well, well. Fancy seeing you, Stan."

"Good to see you, Zoe. Looking fine, too."

"Drop dead," said Zoe. "I'm shagged out and I need a bath and if I'd known I was going to run into the remembrance of things past I'd at least have combed my hair. I'll have a whisky. How's the wife and kids?"

"Reasonable. Who've you been grilling, then?"

"Himself. Funny, I was thinking of you this morning, in a general kind of way."

"I never think of you, Zoe, in anything but the most particular kind of way."

"Huh. There's no need to be coarse."

"I was being gallant," said Stan.

Zoe laughed. "I like you, and you can't say that of everyone." She looked at him, roseate in the sunset lighting of the bar, and thought once upon a time I climbed all over you in a bed in Manchester of all places. I couldn't have enough of you and now there's not a flicker, not so much as a frisson, not a single quiver of the faithless flesh. Oh dear oh dear oh dear.

"I was sorry to hear about your brother."

"Mmn. I can't remember – did you ever meet Frances?"

"Once. Quiet. Good-looking. And a bouncy little girl with a funny name."

"Tabitha. Our Tab. Grown-up now."

"I only met your brother once. He put me in my place at a press conference. When he was chairman of that Royal Commission."

"That sounds like Steven," said Zoe.

The American tourists had begun to ebb from the bar. It was past eleven. Zoe commented that there wasn't an Irish voice to be heard. The barman was Italian. "Joints like this have a nationality all of their own. A kind of territorial Esperanto. Thank God I've been talking to real Irishmen all day or I'd feel like the Flying Dutchman."

"Ever woken in a strange hotel room and had to check with reception where you were?"

"Near enough. Why do we do it?"

"Because we want to," said Stan crisply. "Drink?"

"My turn. Doesn't, um, Sally, mind?"

"She's got used to it. She minds, yes."

"So would I. No wonder no-one ever married me."

"Not for want of trying."

"Cut it out. The age of chivalry is over."

"I must say," said Stan, "I thought at one time Eric Sadler was going to make it. I gather he's being seen around with Liz Harcourt these days."

Zoe gazed for a few moments, intently, at the mirror behind the bar. A mirror with art nouveau motifs painted thereon, in a rather disagreeable green. She paid for the drinks, moved Stan's towards him, replaced her purse in her handbag. She drank the whisky, too fast. "That'll be the new girl on *The Observer*. Ah, these gay young things. How nice for Eric. You know something, Stan, I feel a sudden crazy urge for some fresh air. I think I'll take a walk into town."

"Well, take care. I'd come with you but . . ."

"You get yourself a night's sleep. Good seeing you."

She walked through the foyer out into the street and in the direction of the Liffey. Men spilled from a bar and passed her, with comments that Zoe ignored – barely, indeed, heard. She was noting, at that moment, the intensity of the stars, spiking the city sky with such brilliance that the street lights seemed tarnished. She isolated the Plough, the North Star, Orion, and as she did so it came to her that the last time she had been so conscious of constellations had been in New York, a few weeks ago, seeing them laid out behind the panoramic screen of an office window, unearthly backdrop to the balding head of a Manhattan police chief. That's the kind of thing that keeps people sane, she thought, at rough moments. Constancy. That night will follow day. That the world at least is reliable.

This is not all that rough a moment. It has happened before and no doubt will happen again. And those who are not prepared to give all cannot expect to have all, either. But I am dog tired and fifty next week and I feel as though someone has just given me a light punch in the belly.

She leaned over the parapet of a bridge. A passing man made a suggestion. "Sod off," said Zoe without turning her head. The Liffey lay sluggish below her, oil patches gleaming. I have been here before, she thought, I have passed this exact spot. It comes back now, that quay and this bridge and the Custom House over there. I walked along here with – with I forget who – time out of mind ago, when I had my first job. All keen and bright and pushy, doing a piece on de Valera. Hi there, Zoe. Zoe Brooklyn, then and now. Not so very different, if you disregard the hand of time. We'd recognize one another. And there's consolation in this, too; knowing from whence you have come. That you passed this way before. It wasn't such a bad idea to take a walk; better than soaking up more whisky with old Stan. Not his fault; he wasn't to know. The punch in the belly is wearing off a bit. We can take it. And there is work to be done, thank God, and tomorrow will be another day.

It had begun to rain. She shoved her hands in the pockets of her coat and walked back across the bridge, fast, arranging in her head the opening paragraphs of an article.

After Frances and Harry arrived back in London one or two newspaper reporters telephoned. Harry, stiffly, gave minimum replies: yes, thank you, he was better; no, he didn't know quite what he'd be doing next; no, he didn't really want to talk about the airport bombing. There was a photograph of him in *The Standard*, with a few lines of comment that referred more to Steven than to Harry. The other British casualty, a middle-aged woman from Bristol, was not mentioned.

It had become hot: dusty London mid-summer. Tabitha came back from Cambridge and went away again almost at once to an archaeological dig in Scotland. She was irritable and abstracted. Frances, hurt, asked Harry what was wrong.

"There's some bloke, I think," said Harry, embarrassed.

"You mean she's in love? It's nothing to be ashamed of. She was so furtive. I wish she'd talk to me."

Harry shrugged, evidently finding the whole matter distasteful. He spent his time sitting in the garden reading, or shuffling around on his crutches, patiently waiting for the leg to mend. He never complained. He is doing, Frances thought, exactly what Steven would have done. If he were Steven's natural son people would say he had his temperament; he is pragmatic and rational, like Steven, almost disconcertingly so. But he isn't Steven's son, nor mine, we are just people with whom he has spent his life. He has never displayed the slightest interest in his origins; that, too, of course may be a matter of temperament. Since he is what he is, and has what he has, there is no point in considering what might have been. That also would have been Steven's position.

She visited the new house; the smaller house in another part of London. The house suitable for a widow whose children were no longer permanently resident. Its present owners were a young couple expecting a third baby, seeking expansion. The mother, a toddler slung across her hip, wandered round the rooms as Frances measured floors and windows. "I'm sad to be going, in a way, I mean, the new place is great, there's a real garden for the kids, somewhere for John to have a workshop. But you leave a bit of yourself in a house, don't you?" Frances, looking out on to the unfamiliar street that soon would not be so, nodded. She saw the terrace opposite, its doors and flights of steps and frontages with small displays of personality by way of plants or new paint, and thought of houses as vessels through which people unceasingly flow. Passive, and ultimately triumphant. These houses were over a hundred years old. And doing nicely. The mother set the child down and he began to poke spent match sticks from an ashtray through a crack in the floorboards with tiny, delicate fingers. "Don't do that, Tom. This'll be Mrs Brooklyn's house next month. She doesn't want a lot of rubbish under her floors." The child flung itself at her, clutching her round the knees, and she stroked his hair, absently, automatically. "The neighbours are nice. We've never had neighbour problems. And there's the new Sainsbury's just opened beyond the tube station – you know . . ." Frances shook her head; she had chosen this area for just those reasons: it was unfamiliar, a blank sheet. If Steven had ever walked these streets she knew nothing of it, she had not been with him. "Oh well, it's five minutes away, you can park round the back. Would you like a cup of coffee?"

The subterranean thunder of the underground was just audible; Frances pictured, far below, the seated figures lined up in the canister of the train, hurtling through darkness. Scores of strangers, scores of faces one would never see, sharing nevertheless the same small segment of the city, the same moments of time, the same sights and sounds. And, when she looked again out of the window, the sky too was occupied: one plane crawled slowly across the skyline just above the rooftops, purposeful but leisurely, as though searching for a likely spot to land, while another – so high as to be nothing but a silver flash of light – drew a white pencil of vapour across the sky. She imagined these people also, adjusting their seat-belts, opening magazines, talking in foreign tongues. The strangeness of sharing the physical world with unknown others, whose eyes see what we see, whose lives touch ours and then spin off into a mysterious oblivion, had always astonished her. Once, she tried to talk to Steven of this. She saw now his expression, at once puzzled and slightly impatient. He had not understood her; it was not the kind of thing about which he thought, it did not interest him. He would have found the idea sterile.

When the day of the move arrived she came downstairs early in answer to the doorbell and found Zoe on the step.

"What on earth are you doing here?"

"Come to help."

"You can't do that," said Frances, following her into the hall. "You've got work to do."

"Phooey – it's my day off." She surveyed the packing-cases, the cartons spewing books and papers. "Lovely. I like a scene of chaos."

Frances sat down on the bottom step of the stair. "You've come because you think leaving here is going to send me into a decline."

"If you want to put it like that," said Zoe, "you're at liberty to do so. How about I get the bed-clothes off the beds and take them on over to the new place in the car and get it swept out?"

"As a matter of fact I'm not really feeling anything very much about going. I'm glad if anything."

"Then it's merely a question of nuts and bolts, over which I might come in handy. Where do I start?"

"Let's have some breakfast first. Harry's got his plaster off, by the way."

"Good. And I had a card from Tab. One, mind, in six weeks or thereabouts."

"Apparently she's in love," said Frances.

"Ah. Well, few of us are spared that." Zoe dumped herself on the kitchen chair. "And some of us are addicted. Eric has a new fancy lady, incidentally."

Frances, making toast, glanced at her. "Oh, Zoe . . . But it's not . . ."

"The first time. Oh dear me, no. He'll get over it. She's all of twenty-eight and she has ginger curls. Enough of her, though. I am rising above her. Effortlessly. Tab's postcard was all about things called brochs, I couldn't understand a word of it. And signed Elizabeth T. Brooklyn. Has she turned against that crazy name?"

"It's a joke," said Frances. "She's always rather liked it. She used to say, at least you never meet another."

Zoe scowled into her tea-cup. "My fault. My fault entirely."

"I like it. I always have."

They looked at each other: an old look, a private look. Zoe said, "Do you think she ever notices me glowing at her?"

"She's not all that perceptive."

"Rubbish. She's as perceptive as she is beautiful, talented and intelligent. You know, my love, one day soon . . ."

Frances rose abruptly. "Maybe. Look, I'd better rout Harry out of bed. The removal men will be here any minute."

That night, she lay in her own bed in the strange house and felt, for a while, a resurgence of the panic that had visited her in Venice. She thought, I may have done the wrong thing. I may have been unspeakably stupid. I may have made things worse. She felt like the passenger in a ship from whom the shore slowly recedes. She would live, from now on, between walls that had never known Steven's presence. She would return to what from now on she must call home through a door never opened by Steven. Loss, as so often, gripped her with a clutch that almost took her breath away. She lay staring at the pale square of the curtained window, chilled with the burden of it. And there came into her head suddenly the memory of Ruth Bowers; she saw that ugly kindly face, heard that slightly hoarse voice, talking on. In the first months after Steven's death she had flinched from making any kind of relationship; the admission into her life of people he had not known seemed a kind of betrayal. But in Venice she had felt a satisfaction; even, a small achievement. My friend. And this house, she thought, is mine. Mine alone. I am alone in it.

She held the fact to her, concentrated on it, and presently the panic ebbed. No, she thought, I was not wrong to do this. I have to go on, not stay still. I am not happy but there are times, now, minutes, hours, when I am not miserable either. When I begin to live again.

She lay there, in the alien darkness. Warily, she summoned up one of those moments. Dorset. That hillside.

There are days, which succeed one another, and in which we do what has to be done and in which time runs level; passing, simply, bringing with it pleasure and irritation and satiety and tiredness and all those ordinary furnishings of life. And then, rarely and unpredictably, there are fragments and passages from days which are of another order altogether. They are beyond and without chronology; they hang suspended, possessions for all time. To be called up out of darkness.

She stood on the side of this hill, at the top of which there was a prehistoric fort or something, and the blue day rolled away below her: fields and trees and a sky with small coasting clouds. And the wind blew through her hair. The children were running on ahead, bobbing in and out of view between the contours of the hill. She had thought herself alone, had thought Steven was with them, and then suddenly she felt his hand on her back, between her shoulder-blades. And the touch was extraordinary, as though he had never touched her before, as charged as his first touch, the first time he had taken her hand, the first time he had kissed her. She stood there, without turning to look at him, and he said, "I love you." He who so rarely spoke those words.

There was a kestrel that hung at eye-level, negotiating the winds. And very small brown butterflies on the cropped bouncy turf.

She said nothing. He took his hand from her back but she felt still the print of it (as she felt it now . . . lying in the darkness of another time . . .). She had thought: why suddenly does happiness descend, out of nowhere, like an archangel, out of a day that on the face of it is like any other? How can it be that life is quite unexceptional, and then all of a sudden it is not: it becomes a marvel?

Steven said, "I am not with you enough. I know that. But you must never think it is because I don't want to be. It is because I cannot help being the sort of person I am."

"I know. It doesn't matter."

"Last week, when I rang you from Paris, I was missing you unbearably."

"Yes," she said. "That happens to me too."

They began to walk up the hill. Ahead, above, the children scurried in the sunshine. Tabitha, aged eight. And Harry, seven.

"Just so long as you realise," he went on, "I don't talk about this sort of thing very much, I know. But that doesn't mean . . ."

"Darling," she said, "I know. It's all perfectly all right."

"Sometimes, when I'm in the middle of something, I think of you. Committees. Teaching. I think of you and I know that you are there, that you are always there, and I can hardly believe it."

Frances said, "I love you too."

And later, in the bedroom of a hotel that had faded subsequently to an impression of over-patterned rooms and walls that crawled with flowers they had made love, late into the night, and as though that too were for the first time. Steven had said, in the middle of it, "I'm sorry about being sharp sometimes. And distant. When that happens, please think of this, if you can." And Frances had replied, "I will. It's all right – I do."

All this, now, in the awful solitude of the new house, she summoned up. Deliberately and in fear. Over the last months, that time and others had summoned her, when she least wanted it, when she could least resist it, and she had suffered them, in anguish. She had longed to be without the power of recollection; bleached of memory. Tonight, she sought out the Dorset hillside of her own free will, and while the pain was still there, so also was something else. A privacy. That is mine also, she thought, mine alone. Eventually, she slept.

Chapter Seven

The new house was in that north London area of early nineteenth century terraced houses north-east of King's Cross. To Frances, used to the leafier heights of Highgate and sensitive, as Londoners are, to nuances of change in architecture and the pattern of streets, it seemed more densely urban and disproportionately strange. A landscape that is unknown is also unresponsive; she was walking around now in a place without associations. She was irritated by the nostalgia she felt for the familiar shops and banks and bus-stops and arterial roads from which she had come and to which she had never been particularly attached; to be so vulnerable to place seemed an unnecessary frailty. Determinedly, she stumped this new environment, attaching herself to it.

It was an area hustled by change, ever since the linked villages of which it was composed had erupted and fused with the city. The terraces had mostly been built within ten or twenty years of each other suggesting that at the time the place must have been one feverish building site, and indeed this state of growth and mutation persisted, with piles of ginger sand along the pavements, stacked bricks and timber, the occasional churning cement mixer. Now, those stolidly surviving structures were being shored up and reconstructed and improved and thus hauled into the late twentieth century and a different strata of society. They housed today the youngish middle class. Though by no means entirely so; survivors of another time still brought kitchen chairs out on to doorsteps on sunny days, as determinedly as the cobbles that bubbled up from beneath the tarmac of the roads after a bad winter. And the corner shops lived on, run now by Asians, their cluttered and comprehensive stock of sugar, toothpaste, birthday cards, washing powder and newspapers competing nicely with the gleaming shelves of Sainsbury's and Marks and Spencer. The past does not lie down and die, Frances saw, a good deal of it is regenerative, like those primitive organisms that reproduce by splitting off their more resilient parts.

When she was not thus acclimatising herself, she spent the time getting the house to rights and going through the many boxes of Steven's papers, resolutely destroying everything that seemed unimportant. She was determined that the house should not be one of those overstocked domestic archives in which everything is indiscriminately preserved. She had kept only those furnishings she liked best or which were most useful and set about, now, keeping only those things of Steven's that she felt to be especially significant.

On one of these occasions, kneeling on the floor with boxes and files spread out around her, she was interrupted by Harry. He hung around for a few minutes, picking things up and putting them down again and then said awkwardly, "By the way I think I'll be off again next week. Some people I know are hitching for two or three weeks in France and I thought I'd go with them."

"Are you sure the leg's strong enough?"

"Hitching, not walking. At least that's the idea." He fiddled with the window catch. "You don't mind?"

"Of course I don't mind. But be sensible."

"Oh, *yes*," said Harry irritably. After a moment he went on. "Actually, I've got a present for you."

"A present? How nice."

"Hang on . . ." She heard him stump down the stairs. When he returned she stared in amazement. "Heavens!"

He put the puppy down in the middle of the room; it was brown, with sparse wiry fur through which pink skin faintly gleamed. "I'm not quite sure what kind it is; I think it's a sort of mixture but apparently it won't get very big. I'm afraid it seems to pee on things rather."

"It's sweet," said Frances doubtfully. "But Harry, I'm not sure if I like dogs. We've never had one."

"Only because Dad didn't like them. All right," he added, offended. "I'll take it back to the shop."

"No, no . . . No, of course I'll like it. Thank you. It was a lovely thought. I'm sure we'll be very happy together."

Harry, complacent, looked down benignly at the dog. "It eats sort of biscuit stuff. And meat out of tins. I got some for you to start off with."

"Thank you very much, darling."

"That's O.K. Well . . . see you later. I've got to go out."

She sat down and contemplated the puppy, which was

paddling around on a heap of Steven's papers. It, too, sat, and looked at her for a moment with an expression of, it seemed, subservience mixed with expectation. Its stumpy tail convulsively twitched. Downstairs, Frances could hear Harry telephoning a friend: a terse and worldly discussion about cross-channel ferry fares and the route from Dieppe to Aix-en-Provence.

At the end of the street in which Frances was now living there was a triangular piece of derelict ground, half an acre or more in size, separated from the roads at either side by a crumbling brick wall. Its apex was bordered by the last house of a four-storey terrace, the tattered wall that had once been the inside of rooms showing the hollows of fireplaces and the ghost of a staircase. The level of the ground was several feet below the street; an oasis amid the tarmac and crammed frontages, it billowed with greenery – willowherb and brambles and rangy clumps of buddleia amid which roosted old bedsteads and mattresses, skeletal television sets and a doorless refrigerator. Frances, who as a schoolgirl had seen the waste land of the City around St. Paul's in the late nineteen forties, recognised this distinctive scenery with another kind of nostalgia and learned from neighbours that it was indeed a bomb-site, though no-one any longer knew when the bomb fell or what precisely it had fallen on.

A week after Harry had brought the puppy it managed to slip its head through the collar and shot excitedly through a gap in the wall whence it slithered down into the bomb-site. Frances could see it rummaging in the bushes. At that point she realised the mistake she had made in failing so far to give it a name; feeling foolish, she shouted "Come here!" once or twice. Passers-by looked at her and hurried on. The puppy continued to explore. Frances watched for a few minutes, and then to her dismay saw it settle down on one of the old mattresses, apparently preparing to go to sleep. She called again. The puppy pricked its ears, gave a propitiating twitch to its tail and laid its nose between its paws. Looking at the drop from the gap in the wall down into the waste ground she saw now that in any case it would be most unlikely to be able to jump up again.

I need a child, she thought, an obliging athletic child of about ten who could climb down there and get it for me. But there was no child to hand. And it was beginning to rain. Exasperated, she put her shopping-bag on the pavement and began to clamber through the gap in the wall. The puppy, lifting its head, watched with interest. She slithered awkwardly down the drop and advanced on the puppy, collar in hand; it greeted her with enthusiasm and a trace of reproach, as though the whole situation were of her making. Tugging it behind her on the lead, she set about the return journey. The drop, seen from below, was steeper than she had thought: a treacherous arrangement of crumbling earth topped by the brick foundation of the wall. She tried unsuccessfully to get a foothold. An elderly man glanced down at her and then walked away.

For several minutes she scrambled and slipped back, falling once into a piece of rusty iron which gashed her leg. It was raining steadily; she was on the edge of tears. And then suddenly there was a woman looking down at her, a youngish woman with long lank black hair. She said, "Is there anything I can do?"

"If you could . . . find something I could get hold of and give me a pull. I can't get a foothold."

"I've only got the belt on my rain-coat. Here, catch hold . . ."

When, at last, Frances achieved the pavement she was mud-streaked and soaking wet. The woman said "You've got a cut on your leg. That's our house opposite. You'd, better come in and wash it."

"I live just down the road . . ."

"You're getting blood all over your shoe. You'd better come." There was something at once persistent and resigned about her; she had a very white face, bare of make-up. On the doorstep she paused: "I'm Marsha Landon."

The house, within, was identical to Frances's own, but of such different temper as to be startling. The shabbiness of walls and floors was almost aggressive; plaster was chipped from the cornices, the dark floral wallpapers had been torn away in places, the boards were either bare or covered with fraying cord carpet or disintegrating rush matting. From somewhere came the sound of a typewriter. Marsha led Frances into a kitchen in which the remains of a meal stood on the table and a sink was piled high with dirty crockery. She filled a bowl with water and brought a towel; a not very clean towel. Then she stood watching while Frances wiped mud and blood from her leg; she was, Frances now saw, older than she had at first appeared, fortyish, but with a pale childish face and skinny body. "P'raps you should go and have some stitches in it."

Frances said, "I think it'll be all right."

A man appeared in the doorway. Marsha said, "This is Philip. My husband. Sorry, I don't know your name."

"Frances Brooklyn. Your wife very kindly . . ."

"She lost her dog in the bomb-site."

Philip Landon was in his mid-fifties, a tall man with a long face on which skin hung in folds. He wore an out-at-elbow sweater and trousers so ill-fitting that they seemed hardly to graze his lean body. He pulled a chair out and straddled it, leaning his elbows on the back. The stare he directed at Frances was so disconcerting that she found herself looking away; it both disquieted and compelled attention.

"You're a neighbour?"

"Yes. I came here just last month."

"I'd heard the gentry were moving in."

"We've been here fifteen years," said Marsha. "And it's stupid to talk like that, Philip. Our house is the only run-down one left, just about."

He ignored her. "Anything to do with Steven Brooklyn, by any chance?"

Frances said reluctantly, "He was my husband."

"Well, well. I was at school with him." His gaze, still, was fixed on her; she could not understand why he made her so uncomfortable. "Make us some coffee, Marsha."

"Actually, I must go."

"Why?" said Philip Landon.

She could think of no reply.

"He was very much the golden lad, your husband. Clearly destined for higher things."

"I don't remember him ever mentioning . . ." Frances began.

"No. He wouldn't have. We weren't what you might call birds of a feather."

Silence, unnervingly, descended. Marsha was spooning instant coffee into mugs. Frances, driven to speech, began to talk brightly about the neighbourhood. Coffee, not quite hot enough, was set before her. Philip Landon lit another cigarette; he seemed uncannily at odds with the times, his seediness was the seediness of another era, his destructive cynicism was in some way unrooted. Marsha spoke of local politics; his comments and interruptions, always derogatory, veered unsettlingly across the spectrum of opinion; it would have been quite impossible to tell where his political fidelities lay, if indeed they lay at all. He made Frances think of the fifties; another atmosphere clung to him – afternoon drinking-clubs, cinema queues, duffel coats and jazz played on wind-up gramophones. A recollection, an unwelcome sleazy recollection stirred – not of this man but another, similar man. A smoky room and too much raw wine. A knee thrusting between hers, wanting-to conflicting with not-wanting-to in a humiliating blinding loss of control. Long ago. Time out of mind ago. Time before Steven. She knew now, up to a point, why Philip Landon made her uneasy.

He and Marsha continued to talk of local issues. What she stated, he contradicted or criticised. At one point she snapped, "You don't know anything about it, Philip, you sit here on your arse all day, when did you last go to anything?" She turned to Frances. "He writes."

Philip watched with amusement. "Now you've got the poor woman wondering if she should have heard of me."

Irritation tingled. Frances said, "I don't think I have. What do you write?"

He continued to watch her, smiling. "Books."

"Two books," said Marsha. Spite thickened the air: the high note, beyond hearing, of an old strife, customary and formalised.

Philip said, "Frances's husband wrote lots of books. Scholarly books. Learned books."

"Your books are learned in a way." Marsha tucked a strand of black uncherished hair behind her ear; she was dimly attractive, waif-like, apparently without self-regard. She went on, to Frances, "One of them's about the suffragettes and the other's about those progressive schools in the thirties."

"Did you go to one?" asked Frances – and then added, "No, of course, you went to Steven's school."

"I remember Steven rather well," said Philip. "Interesting, somehow, that I should have known him even before you did. Shall I tell you about him?"

Frances stiffened. She gulped the rest of the clammy coffee. The puppy nosed at her leg and, gratefully, she stooped to pat it and clip the lead to its collar. "I really must go now. Thanks so much for ministering to me."

Philip, his chin propped still on his arms, astride the chair as he had been since he came into the room, made no move. "Why don't you come round for a drink on Thursday? There'll be others. Meet the neighbours."

"Well, it's awfully kind," she began. "But I'm not quite sure . . . I'll have to look when I get back and see if . . ."

"Don't you want to take on some protective colouring? Get settled in. Therapeutic, I should have thought."

She flushed. This is impertinent, she thought. I don't like him. "Well . . ."

"Do come," said Marsha, in an off-hand way.

Philip stood up. "Come upstairs a minute. I'll show you something."

Reluctantly, Frances followed him. The shabbiness of the house accelerated as they climbed; through a half open door she caught sight of an unmade bed, another room seemed to be filled with cardboard boxes and piles of newspapers. They went into an attic on the top floor, Marsha bringing up the rear. It was lined with bookshelves in which books were carelessly stacked, upright and in piles. A desk with typewriter and disordered sheets of paper stood before the window. Dirty mugs and glasses were pushed into a corner of the uncarpeted floor.

Philip opened a cupboard and rummaged around. "Here we are. The alma mater." He laid a photo album on the table.

The photograph, sepia with age, showed rows of boys, stepped one above another. Lines of faces, almost indistinguishable. In the centre, masters sat with folded arms. Frances said, "Yes. Steven had one of those." She looked away from the photograph at once.

Philip leaned over it. "Let's see now. Here's me. Steven of course is a prefect – that's him, isn't it?" Marsha, from the doorway, said in a low voice, "Don't go *on*, Philip."

"I'm sorry, Frances," said Philip, in a new tone of voice, conciliatory, without that mocking edge. "Have I been tactless? I just thought you might be interested." He closed the album. "Look at my view. Right down to St. Paul's on a clear day." He stood beside her at the window, and, as she looked out, laid a hand for a moment lightly on her shoulder to turn her. "No, not that way – the other side."

Frances, her agitation subsiding, said, "Oh yes, I see. It must be a nice place to work." His change of tone had further confused her; another, less abrasive man seemed to lurk. His hand was no longer on her but she shifted slightly away from him. She looked at the grey London landscape reaching away to a pearly horizon; towers and spires rose up fragile from the mass of buildings, like paper cut-outs; a gull drifted across the window at eye-level. But the room was stuffy, rank like an unaired bedroom. She searched for another gambit by which to escape. Marsha had dumped herself down in a decaying basket chair and was looking at a copy of *The Times Literary Supplement*. She said, "Philip, this is nineteen seventy-*six*. Why the hell don't you ever chuck anything out?"

"I sometimes ask myself that question." They looked steadily at each other for a moment and then Marsha dropped her eyes once more to the paper. Frances said, "And I really must get back home to do just that – I'm still in the middle of a whole lot of sorting out. It seems to take for ever." She moved, resolutely, towards the door. The Landons remained exactly where they were, watching her, Marsha in the chair and Philip in front of the window; she thought, in bewilderment and irritation, that they were simply going to remain there and let her find her way downstairs and out by herself. And then, as she hesitated, Philip said, "Well, far be it from us to stand in your way. Nice of you to look in." He spoke as though the visit were of her seeking. In silence, they descended the stairs. At the door Marsha said, "See you on Thursday." Frances, tugging at the puppy, which seemed inclined to stay, murmured something noncommittal.

When she got home she saw in the hall mirror that a button of her blouse was undone, presumably ever since she had struggled from the bomb-site; her bra, and a slice of bare skin, showed through the gap. She thought of Philip Landon, watching her across that stained kitchen table, and glowed with chagrin and annoyance. There was a letter from Tabitha; a rather flat narrative of events, carefully drained, it seemed to Frances, of any information that might actually interest.

Tabitha, upon a peak in Darien, on a hillside on the west coast of Scotland, intensely alone and surrounded by others, silent and conversing with a Swedish boy about violin strings, felt the letter in her pocket rustle as she changed position. His letter. The letter. The one and only letter. She said things and saw things and existed elsewhere. She told the Swedish boy that there was this place in London where strings were cheaper, definitely cheaper, she'd give him the address. She saw the long slack outline of islands in a silver sea and felt the wet ooze up out of the peaty ground. She heard the moan of sea-birds, those cries that would be now forever linked with a certain feeling, with this feeling, with this fracture of the mind that was like nothing else, that was like they said it was in books and yet was not. Books, in fact, lie; they lie through their teeth and tell you nothing. They sit smug on shelves, knowing all, and keep it to themselves. They are experts, they tell it how it happens, with their stories and their poems, but when it comes to the point they have led you up the garden path: Catherine Earnshaw and Tess and Jane Eyre and Dorothea and Anna and the rest of them. Whatever you thought you knew about it, you do not.

The Swedish boy, now, was talking about the broch people. Why, he was saying were they so crazy as to come and live somewhere like this where there was nothing to do but look at the view, and Tabitha laughed obligingly. The Swedish boy was nice; he was studying English, not archaeology, so the emphasis of all this, for him, was on something rather different. He was the camp fool; he made jokes and did not pretend to expertise and deflated, from time to time, the archaeologists, who tended to be ponderous. Tabitha knew, now, that she no longer wanted to be an archaeologist. She thought, vaguely, that she might like to work in a museum, but she was not thinking of the future very much at all at the moment, or at least no future beyond the week after next when she would go back to London and he would be at King's Cross, he had said, he would meet the train, he would be at the barrier.

She sat in the heather, brushing earth from the foundations of a little stone wall, the broch people's wall, and thought about him, which of course she did all the time anyway. Thought, though, is perhaps not the word for a process without language, a process involving not consideration but sensation: the sensation of remembering and anticipating and feeling. Feeling above all. For Tabitha, now, this private internal uncommunicable bliss was merged somehow with the world, with the wiry bouncy heather on which she sat, the glitter of the sea and the cool kindly touch of the wind on her face: a physical manifestation of emotion, happiness embodied.

The puppy, unattended for a while one morning, ate Steven's inaugural lecture. There did not seem to be another copy; Frances, guiltily, swept up the shreds and put them in the dustbin. Harry had gone. It was almost September. She counted the months since Steven's death and saw that time was passing, more time even than she had realised. The city was locked into summer; each sultry day succeeded another, indistinguishable, the trees standing motionless and heavy-leafed in pools of shade, the tarmac sticky on the pavements, the grass withering in the gardens. When she was at home, she left the front door open to get a draught of air through the house; returning from the dustbin she saw Philip Landon framed in the entrance, looking at the letters on the hall table.

"I was just beginning to think there was no-one in. Marsha

wondered if by any chance you could lend us a few glasses for tonight. There seems to be a dearth." He moved inside the house and stood gazing at a picture. "Bring anyone with you, by the way, offspring or whatever."

It was Thursday, she realised. "Yes, do take some glasses. But in fact I'm not absolutely sure that I can manage to come. There's a possibility that . . ." She hesitated; she had always been bad at evasion.

He contemplated her. He wore the same decaying sweater and sagging trousers. "And you're not entirely sure that we're your sort, are you? You'll have been used to very elevated circles, of course. I used to see Steven on the box, with all the intellectual nobs."

Frances flushed. She said shortly, "I'll get the glasses."

He followed her into the kitchen. "You seem to have everything very organised. Tidy. Not like our life-style, as you'll have noticed." He sat down. Frances said, "How many glasses do you need?"

He gestured, vaguely. "Oh – half a dozen or so. Was I being offensive just then?" When she did not reply he went on, "Yes, I suppose so. I don't have the social graces very well taped. Marsha, as it happens, took rather a fancy to you. Incidentally why did you pick this part to live in? I should have thought it was rather more up-market where you were before."

It did not occur to her, at that moment, to wonder that he should know where she lived before. She said, "Because I don't know it very well, I suppose."

"I don't quite see Steven in this *quartier*. Though I understand there are one or two names to drop in the area now." And when she cried out, within, for God's sake stop talking about Steven, he went on, "Incidentally, should I keep referring to him or not? I don't really know how bereavement takes people, never having suffered it myself." She said nothing. He looked at her and then all of a sudden slammed a fist down on the table. "Frances, I am being insufferable. I know, and please forgive me. I'll get back. Thanks for the glasses. If you don't show up tonight we'll take the point. I'll drop the glasses back tomorrow."

He walked out of the house. She saw him going down the street: a lank figure with a slightly shuffling walk. He looked isolated; she was no longer sure if she found him distasteful or pathetic. Now I shall have to go to their blessed party, she thought angrily.

Zoe, in the tail-end of the long summer twilight, looked down into the square where, still, one or two children played. She stood for a while, looking, and then poured herself a drink and went to the telephone. She picked up the receiver and almost at once replaced it. Then she picked it up again and dialled. When there was no reply she put the receiver down and went back to the window. The light, visibly, moment by moment, was going. Now, she could barely see the glimmering forms of the children.

Nearly fifty years old, she thought, who'd credit it? There's some things Steven's well out of – he wouldn't have made old bones any more gracefully than I shall. Frances will. Frances will be a pleasure at eighty. I won't. I could turn nasty, I could. I'll be a savage carping old bag, sneering at the world.

And as she looked out into the thickening city night, spiced with lights, with the dull internal glow of buildings, with the streaming passage of cars, she thought of a beach on which, once, she had run with Steven, their feet printing the sand, the water rising at once to fill and blot out each footstep. Pembrokeshire? Suffolk? Who knows, she thought, who cares? It's the thought that counts, the knowledge, the certainty that once I was thus, once I was there.

Chapter Eight

Frances stood against the window in the Landons' sitting room and talked to an Indian doctor. The Indian doctor lived down the road; his house, he said, was the same as this house. And the same as mine, then, said Frances. The room, like her own, was long and narrow, having originally been two. One wall was lined with books. There was a big sofa, its stuffing leaking, over which an ethnic rug had been thrown as a cover. Above the fireplace, in which stood dried flower-heads furry with dust, was a pencil drawing of Philip in youth; it carried conviction, looked as though it were perhaps by a distinguished artist. Frances peered, but could see no signature. She looked furtively round the room; there were about a dozen people. Philip Landon kept circulating with a decanter of wine. Once, when she looked in his direction, she saw him staring at her. She had been with the Indian doctor for rather a long time now.

Marsha brought up a small fair woman, introduced simply as

Christine. None of these people, indeed, appeared to own to surnames. Jilly, Barry, Sandra, Susannah, Aziz . . . It was like the clinical anonymity of a television programme dealing with those in social or personal distress. Or hairdressers, Frances thought, suggesting not intimacy but a kind of indifference. Christine kept using her own name, tagging it to the end of enquiries. "What do you do, Frances?" "Frances was married to an extremely distinguished fellow called Steven Brooklyn," said Philip, coming up with the wine. Collusion and conspiracy bloomed on Christine's face. She said, when Philip had gone, "I'm divorced too." "My husband died," said Frances. There was a brief silence, faintly tinged with resentment, and Christine began to talk about the local playgroup. "We desperately need helpers." When she turned to pick up her glass Frances managed to slide from her and move over to the window, where Philip was talking to a man in a white polo-necked sweater. "This is Frances Brooklyn, who moved in down the road recently. Frances was married to . . ." "I wonder," said Frances brightly, "if I could have a drop more wine?"

I am going to have to do something about this, she thought. Here and elsewhere. I will not be made to wear Steven for ever like a regimental brooch; he would not have cared for it any more than I do. She made determined enquiries about local facilities, not taking in the replies. The polo-sweatered man was in television. "Not Steven Brooklyn?" he said, "I worked once on a programme he . . ." Frances heard herself forge determinedly on, enquiring about swimming-pools. Philip Landon stood watching her; he had, she noticed, reptilian eyes, slightly hooded. What she could not understand was how against all her inclinations something was established between them: a private intimacy, as though they shared a secret knowledge. He both mesmerised her and made her feel uncomfortable. She felt, in this house, profoundly lonely, as lonely as she had ever been since Steven's death, washed up without defences in an alien place.

And yet, when the guests began to ebb away, she found herself accepting Marsha's laconic offer of supper. She felt muzzy and realised she had drunk rather too much wine. The supper was scrambled eggs, inattentively cooked and served with hunks of bread and a watery salad. The other remaining guests were Christine, who disappeared into the hall from time to time to telephone fretful instructions to a child, and Barry, the television producer. The conversation centred on personalities; an actor was discussed, who lived locally. Barry turned to Frances: "Sorry – do you know Paul?" "Frances isn't used to such raffish circles," said Philip. "Do you find us raffish, Frances?" "Oh, for goodness *sake*," said Marsha. "What a way to talk. What do you expect her to say?" Christine, coming back from the telephone, broke in with a saga about a leaking water cistern. "Philip'll fix it for you," said Marsha. "Philip's marvellous over things like that." She stared across the table at her husband, expressionless, her pallor suggesting that she might be in the throes of some distressing illness. "Marsha," said Philip to Frances, conversationally, "is being snide, as you no doubt realise. She is referring to the fact that I am not adept on technical matters and that therefore we have to spend good money on plumbers and suchlike." " 'It is the duty of the wealthy man'," said Barry, " 'To give employment to the artisan' ". "Oh, yuck!" exclaimed Christine. "Who's that, then? Spike Milligan?" "Belloc," said Philip. "A bit out of your usual line of reference, I imagine."

"Oh, you're so bloody cultured," said Marsha. Christine reached out for the wine: "How's the book going, Philip? I do so admire someone who does what you do. I mean, making yourself go to the desk, day after day." "Me, too," said Barry. "That amount of self-discipline." Marsha, her back to them, piling dishes into the sink, began to laugh.

Frances pushed back her chair. "I really will have to go." "So soon?" said Philip. "There's half a bottle of plonk still." "I'm afraid I must."

He stood up. "If you insist. I'll find your coat."

Marsha had sat down again. The three round the table gazed at Frances. "Super meeting you," said Barry.

Frances followed Philip into the hall. He said suddenly, "I'll walk back with you."

"Oh, don't bother. It's only just down the road."

"I need some fresh air."

Outside her door she began to say goodnight. He interrupted. "Could I come in for a minute?"

The walk back had made Frances feel the effects of the wine. She nodded, "All right. Not for long, if you don't mind, I was planning an early night. I'll make some coffee."

He followed her into the kitchen and perched on the edge of the table. His shanks were so bony that she expected them to click against the wood; he was the most desiccated man she had ever seen. He said, "I won't keep you up. I just need to get clear of the house for a bit. The company, as no doubt you'll agree, was a bit dispiriting."

Frances murmured vague dissent into the kettle.

"Don't bother, Frances. I could see your expression. Christine is a sad slag and Barry is a second-rater who will remain just that. And Marsha and I are given to scrapping in company which is offensive to others and self-destructive. Sorry you were landed with it."

She put the cups on the table. When she looked at him she found his long grey face turned towards her, watching, awaiting a reaction. She felt distaste and pity in confusing conjunction. "Philip . . ." she began.

"That is the first time you've used my name, incidentally."

She sighed. "I imagine all married couples squabble occasionally."

"Not Steven, surely. A perfect gentleman, even at the age of fourteen."

She said firmly, "Milk? Sugar? Everyone had rather a lot to drink."

He moved into a chair. "You're slumming, Frances. Unintentionally, of course. This is not the kind of thing you're used to. And I won't mention Steven again, I swear. I can see you don't like it. I'm one of those bloody perverse cusses who are driven to do what they don't really want to do. Christ – you're right – we did drink too much." He took a gulp of coffee. "Well, you don't have to consort with the neighbours if you don't want to. Truth to tell I don't much myself. Marsha has her cronies. As a matter of fact I detest this place. I detest this country. We lived in Spain for a long time. Sun, cheap booze. God knows how we ever came back. Do you detest this country?"

"No," said Frances. She poured herself another cup of coffee. Her head was clearer now. Oddly, she felt a little exhilarated.

"No, you wouldn't. The sun shone on you here, no doubt. It tends to be a bit selective, I've found. I've never had much joy here, one way and another." He stubbed his cigarette out in the saucer, ignoring the ashtray Frances had put beside him. "And damn all now. If I sound pissed off there's good reason. The Beeb gave me the push last week, thereby throttling the one steady source of income. I had some part-time producing work. Now some young turk comes along and decides to prune the dead wood. Frances, I don't suppose you've by any chance got such a thing as a drop of whisky?"

"I'll have a look."

He was a man to whom failure and discontent clung like ash. Steven would have dismissed him. Giving him a small whisky, she felt again that unease. I don't have to know these people, she thought, I have only to be rude, once and for all . . . She sat down and watched him drink the whisky; he was talking now about a job he had had with the British Council, a contract abruptly ended, a hinted persecution, a betrayal by a publisher – years of work wasted – a failed marriage (so Marsha was a second wife). Tired, she took in the tone rather than the content; it was a tone not so much of complaint as of sarcastic acceptance. He seemed to see himself as someone against whom the dice were loaded; others, unfairly but immutably, would always have the advantage.

He finished the whisky. "I'd better push off. One of us'll look in with those glasses." In the hall, he paused. "Sorry about all the maudlin confessions. I'm afraid you're the sort of person who invites that kind of thing." And he smiled, a rare, almost strained gleam that for a moment transformed him. He leaned forward, put an arm round her and kissed her on the cheek. "Goodnight, Frances."

She locked the doors and went to bed. She was in a state

of intense physical arousal. She lay in shame and misery and endured it, longing for sex, for another body, for Steven.

Zoe stood at the entrance to the Day Room of an Old People's Home in Surrey and looked at the inmates; they sat in opposing rows, in basket chairs, as though about to take part in a debate. One old man was reading a newspaper, two of the women were knitting; most of them were doing nothing. The warden hung at her elbow, talking about the recent rebuilding programme. The Home had been the subject of allegations of neglect and abuse in a local newspaper. Zoe the brisk investigative journalist had spoken all day to various people concerned and made up her mind, more or less, as to the truth or falsehood of these allegations. Now, in the middle of the afternoon, another Zoe surfaced. She said, "I'd like to have a word with one or two of them, if that's all right."

The warden fidgeted. "Well of course, by all means. But you've already spoken to Mr Sanderson about whom these problems have arisen, and Mrs Hampshire. There is no suggestion that anyone you see here . . ."

Zoe walked away from him and along the lines of chairs. Some of these people were very old: beyond, she could see, reasonable communication. Only at these helpless points in life, she thought, in childhood and at the end, are we herded together like with like; there was a strange terse affinity between playgrounds of whooping children and this static, largely silent gathering. She paused by various chairs, making conversation; some of the occupants stared vacantly at her, others responded warmly. An old man had some query she could not follow. "They get confused," murmured a young nurse, confidentially.

"He thinks you're the almoner." Zoe stood by a woman intent on knitting a sock; "I haven't seen anyone do that since my mum used to make them for my brother." "This is for my grandson. I've got five grandchildren, three boys and two girls." "Wonderful," said Zoe. "And four children I had, my daughter's in Australia, the others are in London. Mrs Lawrence here's got three, her son's with the Inland Revenue." The old woman in the next chair smiled and dipped her head. Is it thus that we are defined, in the end, thought Zoe, by those we have brought forth? Is that what it all comes down to? "Have you got children, dear?" asked the knitting lady. Zoe smiled: "I'm not married." "You should get married, a nice-looking woman like you." "Well, thanks, love, but I think I've left it a bit late now – I'm not so young as all that." The old women gazed at her, their vision a different one.

She got into the car and set off for London. Fiddling with the radio, she caught a snatch of violins; she turned the volume up and the car was filled with Bach. A Brandenburg? The Fifth Brandenburg? Tabitha sat before her in that college dining-hall, furiously playing, bravely playing. Now and forever, Zoe thought, that piece of music is latched to time and place, to the particular, to those great glossy portraits, to Tab in that frilly white shirt.

She drove too fast, whipping through the gabled suburban towns. The Brandenburg gave way to something else, and those thoughts to others. Tabitha, in another incarnation, comes prancing down a garden path, the path of that house in Sussex, crying archly, "Hello, Auntie Zoe. I ought to call you Auntie, oughtn't I? not just Zoe. Everybody at school calls their aunts Auntie." And Frances, wryly smiling, says, "Corruption has set in, I'm afraid – the awful hand of conformity." They sit on a lawn frenzied with daisies, gilded with sunlight, she and Frances and Steven, while the children whoop and wheel around them. And Frances looks up and says, "You know, it's amazing, but it works." She says it with wonder, and quietly, as though it should not be said. She looks at Zoe; "It works. We had no right, but it works."

During the early days and weeks of her solitude Frances had come to realise that grief like illness is unstable; it ebbs and flows in tides, it steals away to a distance and then comes roaring back, it torments by deception. It plays games with time and with reality. On some mornings she would wake and Steven's presence was so distant and yet so reassuring that she thought herself purged; he seemed both absent and present, she felt close to him and at the same time freed, she thought that at last she was walking alone. And then, within hours she would be back once more in that dark trough: incredulous, raging, ground into her misery. Time, that should be linear, had become formless; mercurial and unreliable, it took her away from the moment of Steven's death and then flung her back beside it.

Now, in the days after the Landons' party, she entered yet again one of those phases. She was glad to be alone and unwitnessed. There was this time none of that disorientation she had known in Venice; she had simply to endure once more the onset of raw pain. She wanted Steven's physical presence until the wanting was beyond endurance; she sat clenched in a chair with a book in her lap and fought her way through the hours, sustained only by the acquired wisdom that the pain would recede, that it would get better, that it might get better.

It was during one of these sessions, late one evening, that Marsha Landon rang the doorbell.

"I brought your glasses back." If she observed Frances's stress she gave no indication. She put the box of glasses down on the hall table and stood; her pale shabby presence required attention, as though to ignore her were to reject a needy child. She wore faded jeans and an airy sweater against which poked small pointed breasts; her hair needed washing. Frances, beyond caring if she stayed or not, said, "Have some coffee."

"I'd rather have a drink, if that's O.K."

In the sitting room, she flung herself into a chair and stared round. "You've got nice things. Not the tat most people in the street have." The puppy, lumbering from a deep sleep, had come over to nose her leg; Marsha eyed it. "I've always had cats, if anything. Aren't dogs an awful bother?"

"It's my first," said Frances. "My son gave it to me before he went away. As a sort of consolation present I think."

"We never had children. Philip decided it wouldn't be a good idea. He had a daughter by Marguerite and . . ." Marsha shrugged ". . . anyway children are an expense and a distraction, or that's the story. Books it was to be, instead of children, though as you'll note, the productivity level in that area hasn't been stunningly high either. How many have you got?"

"Two."

Marsha had folded her legs beneath her. She looked very thin, washed up on the corner of the sofa. "I used to paint, but that's gone out of the window since we came back from Spain. Philip needs the attic room for a study. Anyway, it's not the same here – dreary old London. God – I wish we were back there."

Frances had poured them each a glass of wine. The effort of doing this – of finding bottle and glasses, drawing the cork – and the demands of Marsha's presence had dulled, for the moment, her wretchedness. She looked across the room at Marsha, hardly hearing what she said.

Marsha said, "Do you think Philip's attractive?"

Frances blinked. "I hadn't thought about it."

"Women usually do." Marsha paused, momentarily alert as though listening for something, and then slumped back. "He's got that old-fashioned thing called sex appeal, apparently. As well as a lot of other things we won't go into." She gave a harsh little laugh. "Of course your husband was a writer too, wasn't he? So you know all about the artistic temperament." She glanced at her watch, and Frances realised for the first time that she was in a state of high agitation. "Sorry – walking in like this . . . Am I interrupting anything?"

"No. I'm alone. I was just going to bed."

"I simply had to get out for a bit. That damn typewriter clattering away upstairs, and the bloody rain outside. God, the English summer."

Frances said, "It's only today it's rained."

"Is it? It feels like for the last month. No wonder people here look like they do – that drab hunted look. In Spain everybody laughs."

"Did you?"

"What do you mean?"

"Were you happy? Both of you?"

Marsha looked away. "Oh, God, I don't know . . . It was different, that's all."

You've never been happy, Frances thought, you poor

discontented creature. And you don't love your husband, perhaps you don't love anyone, perhaps you never have. What does that feel like? It is a condition as mysterious as death. She said, "Have you got a job?"

"I help a friend who's got a sort of junk-shop one or two mornings a week."

"That's not a job. That's filling in the time." I sound like Zoe, Frances thought.

Marsha looked offended. "What do you do?" she countered.

Frances smiled. "At the moment, I'm still busy sorting out Steven's papers, then when I've done that I'm going to see what there is going for a not very well qualified forty-nine year old." Am I? Yes, of course I am.

"If you like," said Marsha off-handedly, "I could help you with this sorting-out you're doing."

Oh God, thought Frances, now what do I do?

The doorbell went. Marsha looked up expectantly. "There's someone ringing your bell."

It was Philip. He looked beyond Frances into the hall and said, "Is Marsha here?" He followed Frances into the sitting room where he stood with his hands thrust into his pockets. "I saw your note."

"Did you?" Marsha stared back, sullen.

"You'd better come home and leave Frances in peace."

"Frances and I were having a nice chat. Till now."

"I suppose you realise you left the cooker on."

"Oh, dear, oh dear, oh dear."

Frances broke in. "Look, I'm going to bed myself in a minute anyway. Philip, do you want a glass of wine?"

"No, thanks. Sorry about this, Frances . . ." He shot her a

look, a furtive pleading look that sat oddly on his gaunt face. "We'll push off. Come on, Marsha."

"Oh, for God's sake," said Marsha. "Leave me alone. I only wanted a change of scene for ten minutes." But she got up. "I'll look in again soon, Frances. His trouble is that he can't stand being alone in the house. One of his troubles." She walked past her husband and into the hall.

Philip hesitated for a moment. He shrugged; hopeless rather than dismissive. "We'd had a tiff. Sorry you got drawn in."

Frances said nothing.

"I'll be off. Goodnight."

After she had let them out she looked out of the window and saw them going down the street, walking a little apart. That girl meant him to follow her round here, she thought. And then – she's not a girl, she's a woman, why does one call her that? What a sad pair.

She locked the back door, returned to the sitting room, sat down at Steven's desk. Those two unnerve me, she thought, I catch despondency from them like some kind of disease.

She laid her hands on the cool leather top of the desk and was filled with yearning. She gave in to it, capitulated, let it engulf her. Let me be anywhere but here, and now, she thought; let me be safely then again. In a different house. In the old house. In the Pulborough house, where it seems always to have been summer.

A summer afternoon, with sunshine falling onto the lawn through the branches of the apple tree to lie like gold pennies among the daisies. Idyllic, unreachable summer afternoon. Except that it is not idyllic because it is filled with black anger, anger invisibly fuming around the flowers and the bright grass and the butterflies sunning themselves on the terrace. Steven sits in a deck-chair at the far end of the lawn and she, Frances, on a rug at the other, and they have not spoken now for two and a half hours. Steven has his briefcase beside him and a stack of papers on his knee; Frances is reading, ostensibly, in fact allowing her eyes to travel from line to line and her hands occasionally to turn a page. The children come and go. Words glitter in her head, like pieces of broken glass: what she has said and what he said and what she did not say but thinks. And all of a sudden she cannot stand it any longer, that the glowing day should be thus infected, that time should be so wasted, that it should go on. She gets up and crosses, slowly, with resentment, the lawn, and when she is half way across Steven looks up from his papers and watches her. She says (sullenly), "I'm sorry", and he says, "I'm sorry too", and she says "I always say it first", and Steven opens his mouth . . . and closes it quickly. And holds out his arms instead.

What is then said has been said before and will be said again. The quarrel, Frances's quarrel, is not with him but with all those people and events that take him away, that scuttle plans, that leave the children (she has histrionically declared) fatherless. The fatherless children gather round, scenting a brightening of the atmosphere that promises indulgences, attentions, and indeed yes the afternoon swivels suddenly into celebration. For Zoe arrives, unpredictable as ever, sweeping in with laughter and parcels and traveller's tales. The afternoon softens to evening, but it will never end, they will all be there for ever on the lavish grass in the sunshine. Tabitha darts to and fro, her six year old boot button eyes bright with excitement. "She's showing off," says Zoe. "It's a good thing we're all feeling so benign. And for Christ's sake get her to drop this auntie stuff."

Zoe and Steven argue: she with verve and passion, he with relentless logic. Tabitha sits listening, or rather watching, her head swinging one way and then the other like a spectator at a tennis-match. She whispers to Frances, "Did Daddy win or did Auntie Zoe?" "Not auntie," says Frances, "Just Zoe. Neither of them did. It's not a thing you win." "Oh yes it is," says Steven. "I did." "You damn well did not," snaps Zoe. And . . . "Ooo . . ." says Tabitha piously, "Naughty words, you'll have to wash your mouth out with soap." Zoe glares: "What's with little Miss Prim here?" "Education," says Steven. "You are hearing the voice of Miss someone at Pulborough Church of England primary school." "Miss *Sanderson*," cries Tabitha indignantly. And suddenly she loses interest and is gone, vanishing into the orchard in search of Harry, of apples, of heaven knows what. Zoe laughs: "I am going to have to mind my p's and q's, I can see." She looks at Frances: "Isn't she gorgeous, though?"

The children come rushing past; they are aeroplanes, or birds, or batmen. Frances nods. She says, softly, "It's amazing, but it works. We had no right, but it works." She feels convalescent, scoured by the anger that has gone, clean, happy; she looks across at Steven and sees that he feels the same. In the end, she thinks, it is always all right. What she feels and what she thinks are welded to the afternoon, to the lawn dabbed with sunlight, to these four people she loves above all.

Then and now. Then, which is gone but inescapable, and now, which has to be endured. She got up from the desk, drew the curtains, locked the doors, went to bed. Dry-eyed, she proudly noted.

Chapter Nine

"Do you love that thing yet?" asked Zoe, looking at the puppy.

"No, not really."

"Bless him, though – Harry. The young bring tears to the eyes, don't they? Come here – guilt offering". She rolled the puppy on its back. "This thing is a he, Frances, he's got a prick an inch long already. You're in for trouble with the neighbouring ladies. Are you fraternising locally, incidentally?"

"Up to a point. There's an odd bleak couple called Landon down the road. He was at school with Steven, unfortunately."

"Unfortunately?"

"Well – he's a bit creepy really."

"Any news of Harry?"

"A couple of cards. You look tired. Are you all right?"

Zoe stood at the window, in a scarlet raincoat, looking into the wet street. "Oh, I'm all right. The weather's foul and I've got *angst* or some other kind of iron in the soul. And I'm getting old. And I'm not going to start complaining to you, of all people."

She turned, and her hair was glittering with drops of rain, diamond drops that snapped in the light from the standard lamp. "You're staring at me as though I was an apparition, my love. Am I such a sight?"

"You're a very welcome sight."

Just as, once, in another red coat, she comes swimming into the clear patch rubbed in the condensation on a teashop window, that place in Gloucester Road: Zoe, darting between two taxis, the red coat hugged to her chin. It is snowing; feeble London snow that dies in black splodges on the pavement.

"Bread and butter," she says. "No cakes. Above all, no cakes."

The doorbell keeps pinging as people come in from the street. "I am in the most bloody awful fix," she says. "Oh, Frances, Frances, I need you, I really do. I want your nice warm shoulder to howl on."

A woman in a green woolly hat sits at the next table, her backview eavesdropping.

"Sick," says Zoe. "All the time. It's foul. I never realised."

Numb at first; then a rush of feelings. Love for her; pity; and something else. Something creeping and hateful: envy. Oh, envy, envy.

"Seven weeks," says Zoe, "or thereabouts. Oh, Christ, Frances, what lousy wretched luck . . ."

"Dan?"

But she shakes her head. Not Dan. "Don't ask. Nobody. Nobody who matters. A stupid damn *mistake*."

Zoe's face. Zoe's funny monkey face all pinched and blotched with cold, her eyes pink-rimmed, her black fuzzy hair gleaming with rain-drops, glittery with drops, red and blue and yellow.

"What will you . . .?"

"Some beastly murdering illegal quack," says Zoe.

No. No, no, no.

"It's no good," says Zoe. "Of course I've thought. Thought and thought. In between throwing up. I'd be hopeless. Poor little blighter. I couldn't cope. And I'm going to Paris. I haven't told you. I got the Reuter's job."

Say it.

"Oh, *hell* . . ." says Zoe.

The glittery diamond drops; a smear of butter on her chin; her eyes watery. Zoe crying, who never does.

"Let me have it. Please. Let us have it."

Oh, please.

And now today a Zoe who is another but the same stripped off a different red coat and flung herself on the sofa. "What *are* you seeing, love, with that misty look?"

"I was thinking of the day we decided about Tab."

There was a silence. "Yes," said Zoe. "I've thought of that lately. Rather a lot. Because of her being so grown-up and complete now. And because of not having Steven any more to be sensible and decisive. Should we tell her?"

"Eventually, yes. Steven always said eventually."

"Eventually," said Zoe, "was curiously imprecise for Steven. Perhaps it was the one thing even he wasn't quite sure how to deal with."

"And yet we have all dealt with it well, I think. Better than I ever thought possible."

"We've dealt with the easy part. With what could be dealt with."

"Yes," said Frances after a moment. "I suppose what we never really thought of, back then, was now."

"Now was unthinkable, then. Up to a point we did. In so far as we could. Steven and the lawyers. All the stuff you and I didn't think mattered. Everything down on paper, so there should be no mistakes."

"Will she hate us for it?"

"No."

"For not having told before."

Zoe sighed. "Then all we can say is that we thought it was for the best. That Steven thought that. That we all did."

"It will change everything. Inevitably. Whatever she feels about it."

"Not what has already happened. Her childhood."

"Even that," said Frances. "Particularly that. Believe me, Zoe. That is what I have learned, these months."

"Then we shall have to cope as best we can. Oh, Frances – I'm craven, I'm not in good enough nick to face it just now. Nor are you. Presently. Eventually."

"Why always are you wearing long skirts," asked the Swedish boy, "when the other girls are wearing jeans?"

"I don't know," said Tabitha, "I just do. I suppose it's a bit silly, on a dig. They get filthy."

"It is nice," said the Swedish boy. "Very . . . womanly." He gazed surreptitiously at Tabitha, whom he found quite unnervingly agreeable, and Tabitha, for whom the Swedish boy barely existed, looked out into the morning, the blue and purple Scottish morning in which people stumped around getting breakfast and seabirds cruised the skies, and thought with joy that one more day had gone, that she was one day nearer to seeing him, one day nearer to that moment when he would be at the barrier at King's Cross. The Swedish boy decided that he would remember Tabitha all his life: her small pale pointed face and the dark hair straggling over her shoulders, forever falling across her face and being wiped aside with an impatient hand, her serious abstracted look and the frailty of her, a small thin girl in trailing skirts like some apparition of the past amid the heather. He said, "Always you are thinking about something. Always so solemn, thinking." And Tabitha, who had not realised that her condition was thus apparent, laughed awkwardly and said, "Well, I'm that kind of person, I suppose. I don't chatter."

The Swedish boy who, despite his admiration, had other appetites, went to find some breakfast and Tabitha continued to wait here by the hut to which the person who had gone to the village to collect the post would return. There might be a letter. There probably would not. But there might be. And while waiting in that comfortable state of not knowing, of hope and expectation (because if there was none her heart would sink and the day would be clouded, the morning would be less bright, the hills less purple . . . While if there was, oh if there was . . .), while waiting she would allow herself the supreme pleasure, the indulgence of recollection. Of going back into particular moments.

There were those times when the world stood still: when he said this, when he did that. Hitched each of them to backgrounds now and for ever sanctified: Oxford Circus tube station, a wine bar in Covent Garden, a field in Cambridgeshire. Invested each of them with wonder: as though you walked for the first time in a country of whose existence you had always known but whose reality was beyond all imagining. I am so happy, she had said once, and had heard the amazement in her own voice.

She sat at the roadside by the hut, her arms clasping her knees, waiting. On the other side of the rough dirt road there was an outcrop of rock, rosy pink rock encrusted with a greyish green lichen, the two colours so wonderful a combination that mere random uncaring nature seemed an impossibility. And Tabitha remembered suddenly Steven; she remembered standing with him in a wood, a wood that must have been a birch wood because she could see still the soaring silver trunks, silver patched with bronze, soaring up into a blue sky. The branches had been bare and on them had been the tiny swellings of the new leaves, and somewhere far above small jewelled birds had darted against the swaying trees and the endless sky. And Tabitha, perceiving all this, the structure and the colour and what was suggested by those small secret buds, had been greatly excited. She had been exhilarated and amazed and aware of some enormous problem – aware that all this could not simply exist and no more than that; that such complexity invited wonder and speculation. How old had she been? Nine? Ten? She had worn sandals through the gaps of which twigs tickled her feet. She had demanded of Steven an explanation. She had turned to Steven who in his wisdom and common sense always knew how things had come about and what should be done, and had required an answer. She had raised questions of God and Time and Death. Why? she had said, and How? And Steven had said he did not know. He had explained that nobody knew; he had said that people argued over these things, that the arguments themselves were as important as the things, that the fact that there were no answers was less important than the arguments. And Tabitha had felt cheated; she had asked for knowledge, for huge significant knowledge, and all she was offered were uncertainties. While above her the trees blandly waved their pregnant branches against the sky.

A long time ago . . . Ten years ago. And now Steven was gone, obliterated, surviving only in such recreations, while somewhere perhaps those same trees rose still in their bronze and silver glory. I don't understand, Tabitha thought, I don't understand any better than I did then.

Distantly, round the bend in the road, there came the car driven by the person who had gone to collect the post from the village. Tabitha's heart leapt; she got up; she waited.

When Marsha Landon returned, a few days later, Frances knew with absolute certainty that she could not have her in contact with Steven's papers. It would be an intrusion, an affront to his ordered and positive nature. In desperation, she steered her into the spare bedroom, where boxes of books were not yet unpacked. Here, Marsha laconically sorted titles into piles according to subject and author. She did so with the air of one conferring a favour, wandering every now and then to find Frances with some query, or simply to stand talking. She was, Frances realised, as incapable of structuring her days as a child, and she hated to be alone.

"Philip was talking about your husband last night. At school. They had some sort of fight."

"Fight?" said Frances vaguely. She sat back on her heels, amid a throng of letters and documents, beset as usual with problems of retention and destruction.

"Not hitting, I don't mean. A row of some kind. I don't know . . . Philip was a bit pissed last night. He's been depressed lately. He was going on about one thing and another. He has this complex about people doing him down. The BBC push-off has been the last straw."

"Mmn . . ." I don't know how much of this I can stand, Frances thought. She consigned a heap of papers to the waste paper basket, distracted by Marsha's lingering presence. Her pallor and her slow way of moving gave the impression of someone from whom all relish of life had long been leaking. "Marsha, I've got to go out soon. It's nice of you to help but I mustn't take up too much of your time."

"Have you . . . sort of got over it yet?" said Marsha suddenly. "I mean your husband dying."

"No," said Frances shortly. "I don't imagine people do. It's a question of getting yourself going again, not getting over."

"It must be worse being unhappy when you have been happy."

Frances looked at her. The remark seemed to suggest unexpected perception of several kinds. "Possibly."

"I'll have to go, actually." Marsha spoke as if she had been impeded in some way. "I'm going down to Kent for a couple of days to see my sister. Philip's going to have to fend for himself. I'll look in again when I get back."

It was the end of August. The year was tipping downwards again. Frances, with the intense awareness of time that she had had since Steven's death, saw the changing quality of the light, that softness of dying summer. Waking in the mornings, she noted the spicy coolness of the draught through the open window; later in the day, tidying up the small garden, she watched the afternoon sun hanging always a little lower above the line of the rooftops, felt its tentative warmth on her face and arms. This consciousness of the physical world had been with her all the last months; sometimes she had felt that she was nothing but a pair of eyes and ears. She had walked about as though she were invisible and mindless, acutely registering what she saw and heard; colours were brighter, sounds louder. And always there had been the tormenting contradiction: whether the permanence of place was a solace or a mockery. In Venice, she had seen that beauty is constant, heartless and quite detached from the beholder. She had sat in a café staring at the Doge's Palace in numb misery and the harmony of light and shade and shape had been exactly the same as twenty years before. And at other times she had seen suddenly the incandescence of clouds piled above a horizon, or the play of leaf shadows on the pavement outside the window, and had been strengthened. In the first days, the days of raw shock, she had thought only that she was stranded alone in an unfeeling and meaningless world; it did not seem possible that the days could march unstoppably on, as they did, that Steven could be gone and yet that she could still inhabit the same landscape, use the same objects, see with the same eyes.

And now it was almost autumn and a finite amount of time had passed and everything was as it had been but immeasurably different. She was both better and worse: she did not accept but had begun to endure; she was looking forward as well as back; at times she was free. But treachery lurked, always: the black hours, the long aching nights. The physical yearning, grabbing like the resumption of a disease.

She wished that she had planned some kind of holiday. It would have distracted, at least. Almost daily, postcards lay in bright slabs of colour on the door-mat, carrying that suggestion that the world glitters more brightly elsewhere, that the sender has achieved nirvana; Harry, in France, Tab still on her Scottish hillside, friends in Salzburg and Portugal, Ruth Bowers back home and weekending on Cape Cod: "I just know we'll get together again, Frances, it was a real pleasure meeting you."

The weather broke. On a day that had begun with sunshine, shafting through the windows of the house in bars so densely yellow that they seemed solid, immense towering black clouds gathered in the afternoon and hung above the city like a pall of smoke. By early evening the light had quite gone and the rain fell as thickly as the sunlight had earlier lain on floors and walls. Frances, feeling the chill, turned up the heating and put on a sweater; in the street, cars ploughed by, throwing up spray, their headlights shimmering in the thick blue atmosphere. The rain, streaming down the windows, revealed constructional deficiencies: she went round mopping up and stuffing wads of torn-up sheets against the worst leaks. By eight o'clock, although the rain had lessened, it was as dark as a winter evening; water coursed along the gutters, there was a small lake in the dip further down the street. The pavements were empty, as though the city were abandoned.

The storm, when it came, was oddly exhilarating. She stood at the kitchen window watching the lightning slash the sky, which was now almost black; the rooftops, against it, a tone darker, looked as artificial as a stage-set. The whole scene was operatic rather than elemental. The puppy, frightened of the thunder, whimpered around her feet; she stooped to pick it up and saw that water was streaming steadily through the crack beneath the door.

The kitchen and dining room, opening respectively on to a small area and a courtyard below the garden, were both a few feet below ground level. The drains, she realised, were unable to cope with the flow of water. Both the area and the courtyard were inches deep, the level rising perceptibly.

She tried to block the flow with old sheets and curtains. For a while this worked, and then the sodden mess burst like a sponge: black, stinking water oozed all over the floor. The whole basement could be flooded. She became slightly distraught, rushing around squeezing and mopping.

And then all the lights went out. She was on the stairs, fetching more sheets, and had to grope her way down; at the bottom she missed a step and the physical shock reduced her almost to tears: she felt quite absurdly demoralised. There is a power failure and a lot of water, she told herself sternly, and I am alone; nothing to get in such a state about. She found the torch, and a candle, and saw that the kitchen floor was now completely covered. She tried to roll up the big Indian carpet in the dining room, part of which was already sodden, and in doing so banged her head on the table. Her eyes, again, filled with tears. Outside, she could hear the siren of a police car, or possibly a fire-engine. Presumably much of the district was in the same plight. Doggedly, she continued to struggle with the carpet. In the middle of this, someone started knocking on the front door. The puppy, which had just learned to bark, did so, hysterically.

She went upstairs, assuming that a neighbour needed her help, wondering if she had any more candles and feeling a rush of relief at the thought of company, any company. She opened the door and there stood Philip Landon, in a battered raincoat, bare-headed, water coursing down his face. He said, "Are you flooded? We haven't got a basement, but I know what happens to these houses with areas." Without waiting, he clattered down the stairs. She heard him exclaim, "Christ . . ." He vanished outside into the area; she could just see him in the murk, his trousers rolled up, doing something with a stick. He came back in and said, "I don't think there's a hope, doing that. Eventually, it'll all run away, but I'm afraid it's going to leave one hell of a mess." She had followed him down the stairs; the blackness of the house seemed less black, she felt now more inclined to laugh than to cry. Philip had turned his attention to the carpet.

"You're soaked," Frances said. "Here – let me find a towel."

"Never mind that. Take an end of this and we'll get it upstairs."

Together they heaved the carpet up into the hall. Philip went down again and she heard him sloshing about with a bucket. "Have you got any more mopping-up equipment?" he shouted. "And some more light down here would be a help."

For the next hour they mopped and squeezed. The centre of the storm passed and they could hear it crashing over Hampstead or Golders Green. The electricity did not come on. Philip had packed the wadding more effectively against the doors and after a while the insidious ooze grew slighter. He said, "I think the worst may be over. We're lucky. I've known people have to be pumped out by the fire brigade. There's some basic defect in the drains, round here." Frances was surprised by his competence and energy; it was as though a second personality lurked behind that cynical and defeated manner.

Her back ached. She straightened. They were both barefoot and she had tied her cotton skirt between her legs to keep it out of the way. She saw Philip staring across the room at her, his gaunt face deeply shadowed in the candle-light so that he seemed gothic, a stone saint. He said, quite solemnly, "You looked like Anna Magnani in that Italian film about peasants in rice fields." She burst out laughing. "Actually," he said, "I meant it as a compliment. I used to think she was wonderful." He continued to gaze at her; she realised that he admired her and that she was stirred by this: the realisation amazed her. She looked at her watch. "Heavens, it's half past nine. Look, I'll be all right now, Philip, you've been such a help. Do get back to Marsha."

"Marsha's at her sister's."

"Oh, of course – I remember. In that case we both need something to eat, and a drink."

She made omelettes and a salad, gave Philip a bottle of wine to open, piled it all on to a tray which Philip carried up to the sitting room. She lit the candles in the silver holders on the mantelpiece; the room, suddenly, burst into conspiratorial festivity. Outside, the rain still fell, but softly now. Frances said, "I feel filthy, I must just go upstairs. There's a cloakroom on the far side of the hall, if you want."

She washed and changed. Her own face, in the light of the candle, looked at her oddly from the mirror: shadowed, furtive, handsomer than she felt herself to be. She was bemused by the peculiarity of the evening, physically tired, no longer certain if she wanted this man out of the house or not. Slowly, she went down again and found that Philip had laid the food and drink out neatly on the low table. He had poured two glasses of wine and sat folded into one end of the sofa.

He was companionable, talking easily and without that lurking resentment. He told anecdotes of his days at the BBC that made her laugh. He did not refer once to Steven. She thought, I like him better than I'd realised, he's not so bad, he's better away from Marsha. She said, "It was nice of you to come to the rescue. I was feeling very helpless and abandoned. Truth to tell I was almost in tears."

"Then it must have been telepathic. I had a sudden feeling you might need baling out. In several ways."

There was a silence, faintly charged. Frances refilled the glasses. "Anyway, I'll get the rest of the muck cleared out tomorrow and all in all it hasn't been so disastrous. I wish they'd give us back the electricity."

"I don't," said Philip. "It's nicer like this." He reached out suddenly and touched her hand. "Thank you for letting me stay. Truth to tell I was feeling a bit low myself. Weather-induced, no doubt – good pathetic fallacy stuff. I'm rather prone to that, which is why Spain agreed with me. Very frail, I know. Life would have been more agreeable if one were otherwise."

"Come," she said. "You're talking as if it were over."

"I'm fifty-five."

"I'm forty-nine myself."

"Well, I wouldn't have believed it. A happy life must be good for the constitution. Have you had a happy life?"

"Yes," she said, after a moment, "I suppose I have."

In the hall, the little Georgian carriage clock struck eleven. The rain gently rustled on the window. She looked carefully round the room, at her possessions, at the Victorian desk and the wrought-iron lamp-stand they bought in Spain and Steven's photograph on the book-case. She thought, please don't touch me again, on no account touch me, or I am not sure that I can answer for myself.

Philip lit a cigarette. "Is it a matter of constitution or of circumstances, do you think? I'm aware of being rather a gloomy bloke, but I've also felt things were loaded against me, which may be shifting the blame."

"It's both, I imagine."

"And who you happen to fetch up with. Marsha is somewhat of my disposition, I'm afraid. My first wife was a more invigorating person. Incidentally," he went on, "the thing that impresses most about you, if I may say so, is a sense of determined survival. Courage, I suppose. Sorry – I don't want to embarrass. I just wanted to let you know. Now we'll talk about something else. Do you feel established here now? Despite the flood."

She sat in silence for a few moments. "No," she said at last. "I am extremely lonely. Still. And I don't think I am especially brave. It is just that there is no alternative."

His eyes, she could feel, were on her. She stared into her glass. She heard him say, "I'm sorry. Up to a point I can understand. Loneliness is something that has come my way, rather a lot." He laid his hand on her knee.

She did not move. It came to her that the whole evening, the whole slightly unreal time – the theatrical storm, the isolation in the middle of the city, the candle-light – was an aberration. It seemed to have nothing to do with the ordinary progression of days. She looked down at the hand on her knee, the hand of a stranger.

Philip said, "I assume that celibacy must be extremely trying. At least, I've always found it so."

She looked at him. "Yes. It is."

When she was lying under him, there on the sofa because she knew that she could not let him into her bed, it came to her that he had intended this since that first time she had been in his house. He did not say much. While they made love – if that is what they were making – he seemed withdrawn, intent. Once he said, "Is this all right, Frances?" and when she replied, "It is now, it may not be later," he said, "I don't mean that. I mean is what I'm doing right. Is that what you like?" She felt his alien penetration, and the greed of her response, she heard herself telling him to go on, she looked across the room and saw dimly the shape of Steven's face in the photograph and at that moment, violently, she came.

Chapter Ten

She had thought it impossible that she would sleep. After Philip had gone she had undressed and got into bed and lain there like a plank, quite rigid, her head on fire it seemed, and then all at once she had plunged into sleep as into a bottomless pit, and slept on and on, until suddenly it was bright day and downstairs the telephone was ringing.

"Tab!"

The line crackled. Somewhere, faintly, Tab's voice was saying "Hello? Mum?"

"Yes – it's me. Where are you? I thought you weren't coming back till Thursday." The puppy was barking in the cloakroom. She looked through the open door of the sitting room and saw the two glasses on the table, the rumpled sofa; the night swept back, shrivelling her. Through the crackles, Tab was saying something about a train.

"Yes. Right. I'll come and meet you. Is anything wrong – you sound funny?"

Far away, Tabitha said bleakly that nothing was wrong. The pips went. Silence.

Frances put the receiver down and let the puppy into the garden. She leaned against the door-frame, watching it skitter in the flowerbed. She thought, in all the days since Steven died I have never felt more alone than now.

The morning shone. It was as though the storm had never been. She went upstairs, dressed in old clothes, came down and set about cleaning up the basement. She worked herself into a state of exhaustion; when she had finished there was little trace of the flood except a thin line of scum along the foot of the walls. She dragged the carpet out into the sun to dry. She scoured the sitting room. Then she searched in her address book for Patricia Geering's number, went to the telephone and dialled. When Patricia answered she said, "I'm sorry to have been so long getting in touch. There have been one or two problems. Your suggestion . . . I don't suppose you'd still like me to come and help you on the journal?"

"I heard about your son, but I gather he's all right now. I'm so glad. At the moment I have a girl on loan from the Registry but she doesn't have editorial experience." There was a pause. "I'd like to have you very much. How soon?"

"Next week?"

"Fine. It's part-time. Did I say? Two and a half days a week. I'll drop you a line about hours and what we pay."

Patricia Geering sounded brisk and neutral. Just, Frances thought, what I need.

It was three days before Philip came back. When he did it was early evening and Frances was preparing a meal. Tabitha was upstairs in her room. Looking up through the kitchen window,

Frances saw him on the opposite side of the street and, with dread, watched him stop, cross, approach the front door.

"Hello, Frances."

"Hello."

"Are you busy?"

"Well," she said, "actually I was just getting the supper. My daughter's back from Scotland."

They looked at each other, he without and she within. His expression changed though not a muscle of his face moved. "Ah," he said. "I see."

"Come in for a minute, anyway."

They went into the sitting room. She sat in the armchair, he on the sofa. He said, "How are you?"

"I'm fine. Is Marsha back?"

"I suppose," he said, "I'm to take it that the other night was an aberration?"

With exasperation, she felt herself flushing. She could not look at him. "Philip, I behaved very stupidly. Could we just forget all about it?"

"You know," he said, "that that is not possible." He spoke with what sounded like satisfaction. "I would have said you behaved naturally. You liked it, Frances."

There was a silence. "Yes," she said at last, "I did. But I'm afraid that wasn't anything very much to do with you."

He got up and went over to the mantelpiece. He stood there looking first round the room and then down at her. He said, "I see. I'm not really in your league, am I, Frances? Not in Steven's class."

"That's unnecessary."

"Yes. Perhaps it was. I'm sorry." He went on standing there.

The silence hung in the room, rank. At last he began to speak again. "I hated your husband. I can see him now, always with the right equipment, his cricket flannels clean, his pencils sharpened, his Latin translation done. There's nothing like a prep school for sorting out the sheep from the goats, then and thereafter. He was everything I wasn't. I was the form outcast, the one who was bad at almost everything, who was never picked for teams, whom even the masters despised. Not that your husband despised me, especially. He didn't need to. He barely noticed me. He was always captain of everything, top in everything, one of life's winners, he could afford to be gracious. But I hated him. I can remember exactly how it felt. I can remember when I first knew I hated him. He was form captain, and a prefect, so he was taking prep. I was whispering – causing a disturbance – having for once some small success as a joker, the insignificant take advantage of such windfalls. He told me not to. I persisted. He called me out, more in sorrow than in anger, I think, and made me spend the rest of the period standing in front of the others. I was tall for my age, taller than him; I can see him still, shorter and neater and knowing where he was going. After a while the others all started glancing at me and sniggering. He looked round. He said, 'Shut up, all of you. Get on with your work.' He came over to me and said, 'Your flies are undone, Landon.' After that I knew I hated him."

Frances said, "You're not talking about Steven. You're talking about yourself."

"Oh yes, I daresay. I tried to take him on once, at his own level. Let me tell you about that too. Every year there was a Fifth Form Debate. It was a big event. The lords of creation on display – the thirteen year olds, those poised for the wider world. I put myself down to speak against Steven. The motion, I remember, was, 'This House believes in God'. Racy stuff – it was a school that teetered on the edge of being progressive. I spoke for; Steven against. I don't imagine I believed in God any more than I do now but I think I imagined in a wild way that He'd be on my side. Do you want to know what happened?"

"No," said Frances, with a sigh.

"He walked all over me. He had me for breakfast. He chewed me up and spat me out. It was a run-through for all those devastating performances on *Panorama* and *The World Tonight* and so forth. I stuttered and forgot what I was going to say and lost by about a hundred per cent. Afterwards I met him in the corridor and he said, 'Well done, Landon'. He meant it, in a way; he meant I hadn't had a hope and we both knew it and I daresay he was trying to give me what bit of credit could be given, for having a go. But it was the last straw. I kicked him. I think I even hoped in a mad way that we might have a fight; I was bigger than him and fighting wasn't allowed so he'd get in more trouble than I would. I hadn't any status to lose anyway. But he did nothing. He just looked at me – I can still see the way he looked and I'm afraid that I still hate him – he looked and then just walked away. I doubt if he ever gave me another thought. But I watched him, for ever after. In newspapers. On the radio and the telly."

"I'm afraid I can't find anything to say to all that," said Frances at last. "It's a pity you ever had to meet me, I think. A pity for both of us."

"I haven't thought that."

"What happened the other night was to do with your feelings about Steven, not any feelings about me."

"Up to a point. What an astute woman you are, Frances. Almost too astute for your own comfort."

And now, she thought, you hate me too. You had better go away and let me try to digest this episode as best I can. She said, "I can hear Tabitha coming down. I'll have to get the supper."

"I'm going."

At the front door he paused for a moment. "Goodbye, Frances. I wish I could think we were going to be friends, but I can't see it working out like that, can you? After this. As you see, I have a certain talent for self-destruction. And now I know that Steven had impeccable good fortune in wives, as in everything else."

Tabitha, in the kitchen, said, "Who was that?"

"Someone who lives in the street."

Tabitha, staring out of the window, neither seeing nor hearing, nodded.

She had slept last night, for the first time since she got back from Scotland. And then when she woke – in this strange house, her mother's house, her home – for a moment she could not remember what it was that lurked at the edges of consciousness, why she could not trust her serenity. She had lain for a few moments watching the light spill through a crack in the curtains and then it had come back, slapping her as violently as had his words when she opened his letter, pouring a cold chill through her.

When Tabitha was a child she had a recurrent dream about a paradisiac garden. This garden was filled with flowers, trees that could be climbed and swings that could be swung on. There was ambrosial food and drink. The sun shone. Its inspiration, she later realised, was probably a song that Frances used to sing to them when they were small, a song about a big rock candy mountain, about lemonade springs and cigarette trees . . . Always, on waking up, wrenched from this dream, back into which one could never wittingly go, she had experienced a sense of outraged loss. A part of what she felt now was akin to that. If she had never known what she had known, if she had never tasted that amazing happiness, if she had never fallen in love, then the state of ignorance would have been perfectly acceptable. There was before, and there was after, which was now. It was as though she had suffered a loss of innocence. She had been in the garden, and was now expelled.

She tried not to remember. She tried to endure and to move through days and to tell herself that eventually it would be all right. And failed, dismally. Memory, she realised, which only last week had been so honeyed, which had been something to take out and savour and relish, had turned treacherously into a torment. It crept up on her when she thought she had fought it off, and brought tears suddenly to her eyes; it rose up in the wastes of the night, and mocked her. She did not want it, but it was always with her.

"I'm afraid," Frances had sadly said, "there's something wrong. I wish you'd tell me." And Tabitha had shaken her head; she could not talk, misery had made her a pariah.

She kept his letter. At first she had kept it in the hope that by some miracle the words would change into other words. Now she kept it because to destroy it would be an act of self-deception; it was in any case indestructible, like the past.

The words, in that treasured handwriting, crawled across the crumpled paper: ". . . shan't be able to get to King's X after all . . . going to Ireland with John and some other people . . . Expect we'll see each other around . . . too involved . . . stay friends." She did not re-read them because she did not need to. She moved from one leaden day to the next; she couldn't believe that people survived this kind of thing; she couldn't believe that this kind of thing had ever happened to anyone else.

Zoe's desk, at the window of her flat, overlooked the garden of the square below. From it, while working, she could see the comings and goings of children and dogs and those who accompanied them; she would stare down, her head full of other matters, and the small colourful scurrying figures were a solace – a reassurance of life. Ferociously active, the desk-bound part of her profession was an irritant. She preferred, indeed, to write in airport lounges, in hotel rooms, in the clattering interrupted atmosphere of her office. But from time to time need dictated that she should work at home and the square, on these occasions, was a compensation.

She looked down into it now. On the other side of the room Eric Sadler sat swilling whisky round and round in the glass. Zoe said, "Since you were last here the spaniel has had puppies and there are two new prams. I like that. Continuity of things."

"Ah. How was Vienna?"

"Vienna was all go. I think I had four hours sleep."

Eric shifted, a big bear of a man, the sofa creaking under him.

"What's up?" asked Zoe. "I can feel it. Come on, tell. Get it over with."

The sounds of children and a yapping dog floated up from the square and in at the open window with the other noises of the London evening and above them Zoe heard Eric Sadler say that he was going to get married. He said it looking at the floor, and when it was said he went on looking at the floor; she thought she had never seen a man look so laden with guilt; she wanted to console him.

"*Why*?" she said, at last. "Why now? Why this one?"

"I want a home. I want . . . I think I want . . . a child."

"I see. Well, you've every right. I can't possibly blame you. Or resent it."

"Do you, though?"

"Of course I bloody well do."

They looked now, at each other.

"Oh, *Christ*," said Eric.

Zoe re-filled his glass, and her own. "Here . . . It can't make things worse and the morning will be hell anyway. When?"

He muttered something.

"I hadn't realised," said Zoe, "about children. You never said."

"It didn't seem appropriate."

"Well, no I suppose not. I'm sorry. I feel as though I've been rather obtuse."

"You've been, always, exactly right. No-one else, ever, comes anywhere near . . ."

"Shut up," said Zoe.

"I mean it."

"I know you mean it. That's why you've got to shut up. Or we shan't get through with this."

"I nearly didn't come. I walked round the block three times. I never knew I was a coward."

"Look, it's me that's supposed to be the loser, not you. Don't steal my thunder."

Zoe had turned her desk chair to face into the room. They sat, for a while, silent. Below, children shrilly chanted. Eric said, "If you hate me, I'll have to damn well put up with it. But I so very much hope you won't."

"I don't hate you. I shan't want to see you for a while. Quite a long while, maybe. And don't ask me to be a godmother. That wouldn't be appropriate either." She saw his face, stopped. "Oh, hell, Eric . . . It's my own damn fault. I should have been different. I should have been marriageable. I should have realised about children."

"I didn't want you any other than you were."

"All the same . . . I've no business complaining."

"Oh Zoe, stop being so damn nice about it."

"I'm not being nice. I'm screaming. But I'm being honest. And keep her out of my way. Her I do hate."

He was staring at the carpet again, as though he might drill holes in it.

"No, I don't," said Zoe. "Not when I stop and think. Not real gut hating. Just the odd twinge of malevolence. Does she know about your bad moods? D'you know – I'll miss them, even. As much as the good times."

"I'm going to miss you too, Zoe. I'm going to miss you one hell of a lot. It's knowing just how much that almost made this out of the question."

"But not quite. Now then, who exactly is weeping on whose shoulder?"

They sat looking at one another. Eric put out his hand.

"No," said Zoe, "don't touch me. That would be fatal."

He drew back. "Could I have another drink?"

"Help yourself."

"You?"

She shook her head.

"I'm fifty-five," said Eric. "I drink too much and I'm overweight. I shan't make old bones. I want a few years of something I've never had."

"I know the why's and wherefore's."

He spoke with sudden bitterness. "We should have married, Zoe, years ago, you and I."

"Maybe. Probably not."

He got up and walked round the room.

"Sit," said Zoe, at last. "Don't say any more. It doesn't help."

It was evening. The light was fading. Zoe said, "Frances is out of that albatross of a house. Installed in the new one."

"How is she?"

"Not so bad. Harry has swanned off somewhere. Tab is back from Scotland." She paused, "Tab has got to be told about things. We both feel that. Soon, probably."

"Yes. I agree. I always thought it should have been done before now. But you know that."

"Steven said not. He may have been wrong."

"It always surprised me," said Eric, "that such an intellectually tidy man coped so well with such a curiously untidy situation. Don't get me wrong – I'm not criticising, you know that. But those who only knew him publicly would have been startled, I imagine. It could be seen as a somewhat bohemian arrangement, and Steven was no bohemian."

"It was a measure of how much he loved Frances," said Zoe. "And me, I suppose. He knew Frances had to have children or go barmy. And at the time it looked humane, not bohemian."

"He doted on that child. In his crisp way."

"Yes." Zoe contemplated him. "I'm just realising that you and Frances are the only people I can talk about Tab to. Now, just Frances."

"I'll always . . ." he began.

"No, you won't. You won't always be there. You can't be. Don't be damn silly."

After a moment he said, "Anyway, I agree that she should be told. Don't worry about it too much, Zoe. You and she have always been very close."

"That may or may not be a help."

The sun, now, had set, and as the light drained, the square had emptied so that just one small boy remained, kicking a ball among the shadowed bushes. Twilight, smoking up from the ground, was answered by the lit windows of houses and the wash of car head-lamps; soon, there would be the full internal glow of the city at night. And in the hinterland between, the no-man's-land at the end of the day, Zoe and Eric sat on in the darkening room.

When Frances thought of Philip Landon – and she thought of him a good deal – it was with an unsettling combination of distaste and pity. She was obliged to take a roundabout inconvenient route to the shops and the tube station in order to avoid passing the Landons' house. Once, she saw Marsha turn in at the gate; when the front door bell went she did not answer it, lurking guiltily in the kitchen.

She fought her sense of humiliation. She told herself that the need for sex was nothing to be ashamed of, that she had betrayed no-one, done harm to no-one. Marsha, oddly, did not seem to come into it; or if she did, only as some kind of accomplice. And the more she told herself this the more there trooped back images of that night: she saw Steven's photograph observing her from across the room, Philip's expression in orgasm – an expression not of pleasure but of furtive triumph. Sitting in that room now, she felt ludicrously as though her familiar possessions, tethered each to other times, looked askance at her.

All that has happened, she told herself, is that I have slept with a man who was taking some kind of adolescent revenge on Steven. It happened because I am sexually vulnerable, which is perfectly understandable and something about which I cannot do much. None of this can damage Steven, who is beyond it all. I do not need to feel so shabby.

She tried to extinguish feeling with rationality. She invited some friends to dinner, continued to sort Steven's papers, talked to Tabitha who answered from somewhere within her private fog of distress. Frances, guessing what had happened, anguished for her, unable to help.

Chapter Eleven

On the first morning that Frances spent with Patricia Geering working on the journal she read proofs of an article which discussed, among other things, Steven's views on the United Nations. Two people came into the office, both of whom referred to having known, or met him. Frances, filing details of books sent in for review, merely nodded. Her typing, she found, was unreliable. She said to Patricia, "I'm sorry. I'm rusty. I'll improve, I hope."

Patricia smiled, showing bad teeth. She was a kind, decent woman, assiduous about her work. Steven had dismissed her as tiresome. He was wrong, Frances thought. I accepted, too readily, his opinion of people. She went with Patricia for lunch at a wine bar round the corner; Patricia talked about the Institute and fretted, apologetically, about an ailing cat. Beyond her Frances sensed a solitary life: the Siamese cat, a flat filled with carefully chosen objects.

Frances had worked for a number of years on an architectural journal. The Institute's journal, more sternly academic, required much the same skills; by the second week she felt confident and found herself setting off for the office with enthusiasm. She decided that her misgivings about working somewhere so closely connected with Steven's world were misplaced; she began to hope that Patricia Geering would say that she could have the job permanently, and wondered how to raise the matter. Patricia's attitude remained friendly but decorous: a working relationship.

It was only gradually that she sensed something awry in the way others at the place behaved towards her. An awkwardness; a neutrality tinged even with hostility; a faint patronage. One of the older secretaries, hovering in the journal office, remarked with a curious prurience, "Well, all this must be very different for you, Mrs Brooklyn." A former colleague of Steven's, meeting her in a corridor, stood around ineptly, repeating that she must come over and have dinner one evening. The Director, coming into the room one morning, kept hoping that she was settling in all right. As he left he said, almost furtively, "So very glad Patricia's been able to fit you in, Frances."

Enlightenment dawned on Frances. When he had gone she turned to Patricia. "That man thinks that I am being done a favour. For Steven's sake."

Patricia, her face an ungainly red, fiddled with a pile of proofs.

"Is that the case?" Frances demanded.

"No. It isn't. As I think I once told you, your husband didn't like me and, well, I had reservations myself – he could be awfully . . . short." Patricia's composure returned. "I asked you – admittedly on the spur of the moment – because I was getting rather desperate for qualified help. And subsequently, I have to admit, I checked up on you. Where you'd worked previously."

"Good. If I thought otherwise I should have to go."

Patricia said sternly, "I assure you." Both women returned to what they had been doing; the office was filled with the small companionable sounds of work – the shuffling of papers, shunt of a filing cabinet drawer.

The practical production of a journal is interesting but not necessarily consuming work. As she read, corrected, wrote letters, Frances found herself uncannily hitched once again to her years on the architectural magazine; she felt at moments as though the furnishings of that time were still there – the children safely stowed away for the day in their schools, Steven out there somewhere in the city, the nub of her life. Her own hands, hovering over the typewriter, startled her: the thinner skin, the brown blotches. Different hands.

In all the remorseless liturgies of grief, the processes through which she had moved as though conducted by irresistible forces, the realisation that had most affronted her was that Steven would be halted, forever, at a certain physical point. She would grow old; Steven was frozen, now, as the man she had last seen. She returned again and again to this; alongside it ran the reflection that she, already, week by week and month by month, was turning into a person Steven had never known.

Once, she had sat alone in the darkened kitchen of their first house, in the middle of the night, with a baby on her lap: Harry, wakeful and fretting. At last he had fallen asleep and she had continued to sit for a while, looking at his small features, the bluish translucence of his skin, filled with the tranquillity of those who have lulled a crying child.

Looking up, she saw Steven standing in the doorway.

"Sorry – I hoped he hadn't woken you." She was nagged, from time to time, by the fear that her own intense need for children had forced them upon Steven.

"He didn't. When you are not there the bed has a blankness that distresses. What was wrong with him?"

"Nothing, really. He just doesn't sleep as easily as Tab used to. Do go back to bed."

Steven said, "I'll take him." He sat down, holding the child, looking down at him. "It seems barely credible that a grown man will emerge from this."

Their two faces that night lay for her beneath their subsequent faces: Harry still with the peeled and private look of the recently born, Steven still nearer youth than middle age. She had stood staring at them, possessive and faintly apprehensive. She had said, "I don't even think of that." And then, diffidently, "What do you feel about him? Or is it too early yet to know?"

He reached out, put his free arm round her. "I feel what you feel."

"Honestly? You're not just saying it?"

"Oh, Frances . . . No, love, I'm not just saying it. I wanted him too."

The baby snuffled; his face flickered, like water under a breeze. It was half past two in the morning. There was no-one else in the world, it seemed, but the three of them.

When Frances returned from the Institute that evening Tabitha said, "Zoe wants us to go round for a drink. She says she's bored and cross and there's someone coming who you met in Venice. That man who writes things about music."

In fact there were a number of people in Zoe's flat when they arrived. Zoe herself bustled about, apparently exuberant. Frances said, "I thought you were bored and cross."

"I'm recovering. Come and talk to Morris. He's been asking about you."

Frances had almost forgotten about him. And now his face – the pointed furry beard, the rather melancholy brown eyes – prompted a response that was purely reflexive: positive. She realised with surprise that she must have liked him more than she knew. They began to talk about Venice; not about murderous children nor about the treachery of beauty that does not acknowledge the feelings of the observer, but about a picture of St Jerome in his study with a little white dog before which, in that inflamed week, Frances had experienced her only moment of pleasure. And then, Venice disposed of, she told him about her new house, and the job, and he told her about the progress of his book and his problems with compiling such things as bibliography and index. "I'm a mere journalist," he said. "I've never had to deal with these refinements before."

"I once did an index for Steven," said Frances. "It's not so difficult. The thing is to have all these little cards . . ." Morris Corfield nodded gravely as she talked, appearing to take careful note. The conversation, it occurred to Frances, was becoming somewhat banal. She said, "All this is rather dull." Morris nodded in acquiescence and then jumped slightly.

"Not at all. Absolutely not."

Frances laughed. "You were getting a glazed look."

"I was concentrating," he said. His tone had the defensiveness of a child caught out in a moment of inattention. He seemed, indeed, a more vulnerable and less assured man than she remembered. The dinner in Venice came back, with a vague power to disconcert. Then, her impression had been of someone amiable, level-headed and a little detached. And I said all sorts of things, she thought, I wasn't myself at all.

She looked across the room and caught sight of Tabitha, washed up against a wall, looking bleak. "We must go. It's been nice to see you again. I'm afraid I was in rather a bad state last time we met. You were very kind."

"It was a pleasure."

"Well . . . Thank you." She began to move towards Tabitha.

"You're looking very much better," said Morris.

"I am better." Frances glanced across the room. "I must rescue Tab. Goodbye."

Morris seemed about to launch another remark and then said, "Goodbye."

Zoe, alone, opened the window to the dark blue noisy London night. She stacked the empty glasses beside the kitchen sink and closed the door on them. She went back into the sitting room and sat in the armchair looking out at the square of sky across which tracked a red and white winking jewel. She finished off a bowl of peanuts and watched the jewel disappear into a black wing of cloud and wished that she had gone back for supper with Frances and Tabitha, as suggested.

All right, she thought, let's look it in the face. I am missing Eric. I am missing Eric more than I would ever have believed possible. Here am I, who believed herself self-sufficient, who built a fortress around her independence, and now I am sufficient unto myself and I am lonely. In my way, I loved him, and now he is not there I know that I needed him. You have only yourself to thank, Zoe; as our mum used to say, time out of mind ago, of rather lesser griefs. You brought it upon your own head, dear. And yes, I have brought things upon my head all my life, out of risk and out of carelessness. So don't complain.

She sat on in the darkened room, travelling in melancholy from one image to another. She saw Eric, heard his voice, and the sense of deprivation ground into her. She revisited other loves and other miseries, and took stock. I shall get through this, she thought, because I shall grit my teeth and put up with it, but I would rather go to sleep for six months. For the first time in my life I would readily give up a chunk of it in exchange for absolution from distress. I have always reckoned on a fair share of that – swings and roundabouts, rough with smooth – but just now I feel somewhat less well equipped.

Morris Corfield, arriving in time for the second half of a concert in the Purcell Room, achieved his seat and realised that he was in danger of falling asleep – the effect not of the orchestra but of drink. He had always been uncomfortably susceptible to alcohol; in youth, it had made him more drunk than other people, nowadays he tended to become comatose. He coasted through the first piece (some sprightly Vivaldi, by good luck), gathered himself sufficiently to make a note or two, and settled down for the Brandenburg.

By coincidence, the fifth. At once, the English Chamber Orchestra faded from before his eyes and its place was taken by that student orchestra, gamely playing away beneath the uncomprehending portraits. Their faces, now, were not to be recovered, except for that of his own son Mike and the girl Tabitha of whom he had caught sight again this evening, while talking to her mother. And, as Frances Brooklyn's face now dominated, he detached himself further yet from the Purcell Room and the ECO, till only Bach continued to unite them. In his mind's eye, he continued to talk to this agreeable woman. He said various things for which there had not been the opportunity an hour ago. He hoped to see her again. He remembered, in Venice, the impression she gave of someone determinedly enduring some kind of nightmare; he had felt, in the face of it, inadequate. And, since, he had wondered if her confidences at dinner – deeply uncharacteristic, he suspected – would have made him uncongenial to her. We do not always cherish those to whom we have unburdened ourselves. But, just now, she had seemed perfectly pleased to see him and had barely referred to the occasion. They had talked of quite other things. She had given him some guidance about indexing, of which she apparently had experience, and he had tried to give the impression of taking note while searching for some way to ensure another meeting. Consequently, he could no longer remember what she had said about indexing.

Morris was a less confident man than was realised, either by friends or foes. Behind the professional aplomb and a manner that could verge on urbane, there lurked uncertainties. When he was young he could never entirely believe that people liked him; as time passed a reassuring bank of friendships more or less convinced him that they did, but he could not quite see why. He felt himself to be somewhat unapproachable, through no desire of his own, and personally unattractive. He had never cared for the face and form that he saw in the mirror. The first time that he found himself loved, he had been quite genuinely astonished. And when, towards the end of his marriage, his wife had told him once in a bleak and cruel moment of revelation that she had never really enjoyed sleeping with him, he had nodded in acquiescence. It was only later that the remark had penetrated, subtly and hideously re-adjusting the twelve years of shared lives. For a while, after her departure, his uncertainties had so powerfully surfaced that he had become reclusive. Now, alone for years, he had recovered some self-esteem, if not a normal ration. He had almost, once, re-married, but had drawn back at the last moment, realising that what he mistook for love was an altogether more pallid emotion; which might of course have done quite well, but he retained still a sad hunger for something better.

The concerto ended. In the foyer, Morris found himself alongside a couple of acquaintances and paused for a few minutes conversation. Thence he passed out into the bright fairyland of the Embankment: the incandescent buildings, the jewelled bridges, the dark secret gleam of the river. He stood at the parapet, looking, gripped by pleasure; what he saw and what he felt fused into a sensation of elation and gratitude. He was glad to be alive, in that place, with those sights before his eyes; the world, in that moment, seemed to be promising him something.

Tabitha sat reading, day by day. Ranged in front of her on the desk in her room, this strange new room in the new strange house, were three neat piles of books. Every morning she sat down and took one of these, opened her notepad, and began to read. Then a battle ensued between the words before her and her own leaden and thunderous thoughts; on good days the words won and Tabitha travelled with them page by page and chapter by chapter; on bad days she sat, her head churning, and the words might as well have been in Chinese for all the sense they made. From time to time Frances would softly knock and put her head round the door, offering coffee or fruit juice. Tabitha would look up and smile and shake her head and say she was fine, thanks, she'd be down presently.

When she was a child, aged ten or so, she had gone through a religious phase, much taken suddenly with the alien ritual of morning service in the stone-and-flower smelling church of the place in which they were then living. She had gone to a service with her best friend's family and had sat in the envious trance of an outsider; returning, she had smouldered in her agnostic home. "I want to go to church on Sundays," she had said to Steven, glowering. And Steven, of course, had replied with liberalism and rationality that she must by all means go to church on Sundays if she wished, but that it would not be possible for him to go with her. He explained why not. He explained why he didn't believe in God. But other people, he said, think quite otherwise; you will have to make up your own mind, when you are older, what you feel about it. I am sure that Susie's parents would be quite happy for you to go with them to the service. And Tabitha had scowled, while resentfully perceiving that he was reasonable; she wanted to be part of an ordinary church-going family, done up in best clothes, shaking hands with the vicar, gossiping in the churchyard. Frances, taking pity on her, had accompanied her twice and then had said apologetically, "I'm sorry, darling, I'd rather not. I feel silly, you see."

And so Tabitha for several weeks had gone to church on Sunday mornings with Susie's family, returning home in a state of defiant grace, shooting glances at Steven and Frances, who obligingly adjusted weekend plans so as not to interfere with this new practice. And then the church pews had become rather hard and the services longer than she had thought and her relationship with Susie began to creak a little and presently she stopped going to church. Nobody remarked on this and life went on exactly as before. And now, she realised, her beliefs – or absence of beliefs – were much as Steven's, though probably less deliberately arrived at.

Three days after he died, Frances had said to them – to her and to Harry and to Zoe – "I wish I was a Christian." Only Zoe had nodded, in apparent understanding.

Now Tabitha, doggedly ploughing her way through the days, thought that she understood. What I am feeling, she thought, is nothing at all compared to what she has been feeling, I know that. But I am wretched in a way that I did not know it was possible to be wretched. Surely, if believing in God does anything for people, it helps them through things like this?

Then, back with the books, with the huge impersonal problems of the past, she felt small and peevish, beating her fists against impervious windows. All this has happened to everyone, she thought. Not that that helps.

Frances, driving up on to the Westway, contemplated the day ahead with resignation. In the last ten months the mandatory visits to her mother and her mother-in-law, living respectively in High Wycombe and Marlow, had been among the most exacting moments. Both women, widowed, had in their different ways tried to claim community of suffering; Frances had found herself driven into a resentful resistance. She did not want to discuss the processes of bereavement with her mother, or share her grief with Steven's. She felt guilt at her irritation, and the guilt sent her at regular intervals along the Westway, in expiation.

Mrs Brooklyn sat in the farthest corner of the sofa, as though in retreat from her visitor, knitting. She said, for the second time, "I hope you had an easy drive down, dear." And then, "You'll give my love to the children, won't you?" Appropriately affectionate messages, Christmas and birthday presents had been, on the whole, the extent of her relationship with Harry and Tabitha; they evidently alarmed her in the way that her own children had alarmed her. Both she and her husband, Frances thought, would have gladly done without the provocations of parenthood; their purpose in life, if such it could be called, had been to exist as unexceptionally and as unobtrusively as possible. Steven used to say that their most fervent injunctions had been that he and Zoe should not attract attention to themselves.

And from that nerveless upbringing had emerged Zoe, and Steven. Frances, thinking of this, smiled. Her mother-in-law looked across at her with mistrust. "Keeping well, are you? I always say, moving house is a terrible strain."

You haven't moved house for forty years, thought Frances. The room depressed her unutterably, as it always had. All the furnishings were chosen for neutrality of effect or qualities of endurance; a limp beige colour predominated. She got up. "Can I have a look round the garden?"

Together, they toured the lawn and the symmetrical semi-circles of the flower-beds, in which standard roses were strapped to posts like prisoners awaiting execution. Mrs Brooklyn re-iterated how difficult it was to keep it as her husband had liked it; a boy came in on Saturdays, but was not to be trusted. In the circular central bed, clumps of lobelia alternated with red salvia, as they had done ever since Frances could remember. French marigolds burned beside the small terrace. Frances, determinedly, related the contents of Harry's last letter from France. Steven had found it difficult to love his mother; his attitude towards her had been a mixture of duty and an irritated tolerance. Frances, more than ever, felt a bewildered gloom that she should be tethered to this woman with whom she had nothing in common except the fact that she had borne two people she loved. And in whom there seemed to be nothing of her.

She said, "Zoe had a very good article in *The Sunday Times* – about the Vienna conference."

Mrs Brooklyn stooped to twitch a weed from the scoured bed. "I don't often see the papers. We used to enjoy watching Steven on the television. Mrs Rogers next door was saying only the other day he had such a presence. She always used to pop round when she noticed he was going to be on, in case I'd not seen."

Frances said with sudden quiet rage, "Zoe is very highly thought of, you know."

Mrs Brooklyn looked up, catching the tone and instinctively heading away from trouble, "Oh, she's done very well. Harold always said, Zoe's done very well, you know. It's a shame she's never married."

"Zoe has never wanted to be married."

"Yes," said Mrs Brooklyn obscurely. She moved on, pointing out a dying apple tree. "I'm wondering if Harold wouldn't have wanted a new one in there. She always knew her own mind, of course, even as a little girl."

Frances moved away. She walked to the far end of the garden

and stood looking at the fence, precisely at eye-height, which shielded this garden from the neighbouring one. She had never been able to decide if the colourlessness of her mother-in-law's utterances reflected a state of mind or simply a determined resistance to the demands of life. Did she actually feel less, having devoted herself to avoiding stress? She had seemed to grieve at Steven's death, but what she had said, over and over again was, "It should never have happened."

Mrs Brooklyn came up. Frances, suffering a mixture of irritation and guilt that had the odd effect of making her tingle, as though mildly electrified, asked about some old photographs she wanted to have copied. They went back into the house. Mrs Brooklyn, taking the albums from the bottom of the sideboard, laid them on the table. "Why don't you just take the ones you want for yourself, dear. Going to all that bother of having them copied . . ."

"It isn't a bother. And you should have them. The ones of Steven and Zoe as children."

"I've got my memories," said Mrs Brooklyn. "Well, just as you like." She picked up her knitting. Frances began to leaf through the albums, removing a snapshot here and there. She passed through infancy and schooldays and reached student days: Zoe tousled and laughing on a sunlit lawn, Steven in a duffel coat, with odd dapper sleek hair. Steven and Zoe together, looking bored. Steven with another girl, the photo over-exposed, the girl's face too dark to make out.

She said, "I don't remember this one. Who is that?"

Mrs Brooklyn peered. "I think that would be Sarah. Yes, it must be Sarah."

"Sarah?"

"Sarah Hennings. Steven's fiancée."

Frances blinked. She picked the album up and looked more closely. She prised out the photograph and turned it over. On the back was pencilled, faintly 'May 1952'. Three years before she had met Steven. She stared again at the photograph: Steven looked young and grave, the girl's expression was quite lost. They stood side by side in some dark leafy place; the girl's hand, it was just possible to make out, lay lightly in Steven's.

She said, "I've never heard of her."

Mrs Brooklyn lowered her knitting; for an instant a tiny shaft of prurient interest lit her eyes. She said, "I'd have thought he'd have said. They weren't engaged all that long. She was a nice girl. But they didn't always hit it off I suppose and it came to nothing." She spoke as though of distant acquaintances.

Frances returned the photograph to its place on the page. She said, "Now I come to think of it, I believe he did once mention something." She turned over further pages, selected a couple more photographs, gathered together her pile, found in her handbag a used envelope into which to put them. "I'll let you have these back next time I come. The house is looking quite organised now. It's time you came to see it."

"Yes," said Mrs Brooklyn. "I'm planning to do that." Both of them knew that she would not. She came with Frances to the door and stood there watching as she got into the car and started the engine. At precisely the right moment, as the car moved off, Mrs Brooklyn raised her hand to wave; Frances had no idea, she realised, whether her visits pleased the old woman or not.

Her own mother, forty-five minutes later, poured tea, slipped off her shoes and settled to talk. Frances, from whom a minimal response was all that was required, sat supine, not thinking, in that no-man's-land that precedes reaction. From time to time she returned to the photograph, saw it again, turned it over again and re-read the date. Her mother was recounting plans for re-decoration of her bedroom: ". . . very pale pinky-grey walls and new curtains I've ordered with bluey-green flowers." Always inclined to plumpness, she was now fat, overflowing softly into the crannies of the armchair, her ankles puffy, her chin rolling down into her neck. But her clothes were girlish, as they always had been, and her fingernails painted pearl-pink. The room was too warm; comfort had always been the signature of this house – a nice fire, a lovely hot bath. The carpets were deep and the curtains thick; whatever went on in the world, went on beyond them. Years ago, Frances had said to Steven, "In fact, our mothers are not unalike, though neither of them would recognise that."

". . . and a sweet lacy bedcover I found at John Lewis. And I'm having those Redouté flower prints framed that Daddy never liked very much. Chokky bikkie, darling?"

Frances remembered Steven's observation, in a moment of asperity, that a whole thesis could be written on the semantics of speech as a reflection of personality, using her mother as a model.

"Did you say you were going to see Mrs Brooklyn?"

"I've been."

Her mother slipped a cushion behind her head. "How was she? Poor thing, I thought she looked awfully washed out that time I saw her at Christmas. Of course, I expect she has a bit of a dull time." She looked across at Frances. "And now, darling, tell me how *you're* really feeling in yourself."

"Not too bad."

Her mother sighed. "Well, you know I'm the one person who knows and understands. And I still think you should have come here for a bit. After Daddy died the horridest part of all was waking up in an empty house in the mornings. You see, I do so know what it's like, other people simply can't imagine. And now all this moving house . . . I still think that was silly. They asked you to stay on till next year."

"It was far too big for me on my own." Frances put her cup down. "I'll have to go – I told Tab I'd be back by seven."

"I've got a tiny bit of a bad back today," said her mother. "So I won't come out to say bye-bye. You will look for that cream braid for me?"

"Yes, mamma."

"Harrods, I should think. Or failing there, Peter Jones."

"Yes."

Frances drove back to London, along the motorway and then packed tight in the traffic that poured back into the city as though by suction, shoals of cars surging up on to the Westway, sailing above the rooftops, riding among the tower-blocks. The flow sank to a crawl and she sat amid this metal, these trapped bodies, and the photograph printed itself on the windscreen in front of her: perfectly polite but entirely insistent. The kaleidoscope was twisted, the pattern of the past re-assembled, all previous image lost for ever.

Chapter Twelve

"Who was Sarah Hennings?"

"Sarah what?" said Zoe, "I dunno. Oh, good grief, yes I do. That girl of Steven's, centuries ago. Whatever brought her up?"

"Steven's fiancée."

There was a pause. A typewriter clattered. Zoe, voice muted, turning evidently from the phone, said, "O.K., Tim, with you in a minute." She returned. "What's all this, Frances? Why her, suddenly? Yes, they were engaged, now I come to think of it. Didn't you know?"

"No."

"Well, so what?" said Zoe, almost crossly. "It was years before you and he ever met. She's a blank as far as I'm concerned – I don't even remember what she looks like."

"There's a photo of her in one of the albums at Marlow."

"Well, it's passed me by, if there is."

"He never mentioned. That they were engaged. I must have seen the photo before and just thought she was some friend. I think he did once say something about a Sarah, but as though she was just . . . anyone."

There was silence for a moment. "Frances," said Zoe, "This is crazy. You're going on as if you'd unearthed some massive infidelity. She was a girl he didn't marry, long before he met you. If he never said then presumably he had his reasons, being Steven. Presumably because he didn't think it was important. When were you at Marlow?"

"Yesterday. She seemed fine."

"You're a saint – I haven't been there for a month. Listen, you're not really brooding about Sarah Hennings, are you? She doesn't matter."

Frances paused. "I'm afraid she does. She matters to me, and there isn't anything I can do about that."

Later, she took the puppy out for a walk on Hampstead Heath. She walked for two hours, and tried, during that time, to absorb this jolting, disturbing fact. A person is a fact. Everything – each day, each moment – had to be adjusted to accommodate the distant shadowy figure of this girl. This once-girl. Am I jealous? Frances asked herself. Why did Steven never speak of her? Because, as Zoe says, he thought it was neither here nor there? Yes, when I search hard, there were times when he spoke of a Sarah. Casually. What I didn't know was that they were to marry; that they stood once against a background of privet or possibly laurel, holding hands. And now I shall never know any of the answers, because Steven cannot tell me – who would have done, had I asked – and goodness knows who or where this woman is now, and unhinged as I am at this moment I am not quite unhinged enough to seek her out.

She scrutinised what she felt; she picked at her distress and held it up to the light and laid it out for dissection. What mattered was the sense of intrusion. Always, unknown, there had been this episode, lying like an unseen rock under the surface of the sea. However unimportant, it had been there, in Steven's head and not in hers. Why didn't you tell me? she said, now, to the sparkling morning air and the trees and the bright grass, and Steven, a long time ago, replied: Frances, sometimes you are possessive.

She came home, disconsolate, obsessed. She knew that what she felt was irrational and paranoic and knowing this was of no help at all. When the certainties of the past are tampered with, reason itself dissolves. She wondered, wretchedly, if she were in for another spell of madness, as in Venice. She noted, too, that still, day by day, the content of her life was dominated by what had been rather than what was. Even that miserable business with Philip Landon, she thought, was to do with Steven, not me.

Tabitha, coming into the room, stood for a moment looking at Frances who was kneeling on the floor riffling through a box of papers, a curious expression on her face, almost of savagery. She looked up with a start.

"Tab . . . you made me jump!"

"Sorry, I thought you'd heard me." Tabitha loitered, picking up a heap of newpaper clippings. She said, "Goodness, what a lot of *stuff* . . ."

"That's what a life seems to amount to. A great many bits of paper."

"Shall I help?"

"Thanks – but I've got a sort of method which is probably impenetrable to anyone else." She sounded abstracted, and sat staring down at a ring-file of handwritten notes. Tabitha, looking over her shoulder, said, "Undergraduate essays. He never threw anything away, did he?"

Frances slammed the file shut. "Selected items, evidently." She bit her lip, began to sort through a bundle of letters.

"Are you looking for something in particular?"

"No," said Frances, snapping. "Just sorting."

Tabitha, faintly offended, changed her tone. "By the way, I forgot – a man telephoned when you were out. Someone called Morris Corfield. He said he'd ring again."

There was nothing: no letter, no postcard, no mention. No evidence. An absence which proved nothing, and was neither solace nor provocation.

During the days that passed the two women, Tabitha and Frances, lived together and profoundly apart. At meal-times they talked, determinedly, and when they passed one another on the stairs or in the hall of the small house they exchanged smiles of guilt. Each felt that she betrayed the other with her preoccupation; neither felt able to penetrate the other's purgatory. Tabitha continued to tell herself, uselessly, that her own plight was trivial and universal; Frances blamed herself for inadequacy in being unable to counsel or console. They were like invalids in neighbouring hospital beds, slung about the apparatus of their own disease. Both thought of Steven and mourned the loss of his objectivity and calmness; both recited to themselves what he would have said, how he would have advised. They loved one another, and found the love embarrassing.

On an afternoon of brooding September heat, when the city seemed to lie numbed and static at this hinge of the year, Tabitha, unable to bear the sight of her books any longer, went out into London. She got on to a bus, almost at random, and sat on the top deck looking down at the crowded pavements and the office blocks and the sober enduring façades of eighteenth century houses. In Gower Street, as the bus halted at a traffic light, she looked along Great Russell Street and saw the zebra crossing in front of the British Museum, across which she and he had once walked hand in hand. He had been wearing jeans and a blue shirt; she, the skirt that she had on now. The happiness of that day seemed to give the place a mocking clarity: the bright stucco of the buildings, the swaying green of a tree, the orderly black railings of the museum. She looked, unable not to, and it was as though she saw, with the eyes of inexorable experience, a ghost of herself; thus she remembered recently meeting the eyes of the five year old Tabitha in the photograph on Frances's dressing-table: eyes that did not know, and did not wish to, and to which there was nothing to be said. The bus jerked into motion again, leaving the place behind, and Tabitha was carried on towards the clamour of Oxford Street, a leaden weight within her, wondering for how long everything she saw and heard would be thus blighted, how people exorcise their landscapes, how they go on walking a world which does not allow anything to be forgotten.

She left the bus, went into a shop in which music sobbed from the walls, and bought a shirt. She would have liked to buy a skirt and throw away the one she wore, with its tormenting associations, but she did not have enough money. She got on to another bus and travelled to the park, where she walked for a while on the dusty grass, looking at the dark stooping shapes of the trees, the running dogs and leaping children. She sat for a while in a deck-chair. She walked again, across into Kensington Gardens. She examined the Albert Memorial and stared at the hulk of the Albert Hall and then, on an impulse, seeing that the afternoon had slid into early evening, she went into a telephone kiosk and dialled Zoe's number.

"What happened?" said Zoe. "Did he just bugger off?"

Tabitha nodded. "Sort of."

Zoe sighed. "You poor love." She got up and stood looking out of the window. "Likewise," she said, but Tabitha did not hear this, nor had it been intended that she should. "Lousy, isn't it? You know something?" – she turned back to Tabitha – "Eventually it won't matter. It simply will not matter. You wouldn't believe how little it will matter. Remember having measles?"

"No."

"Exactly."

"It's hardly the same thing," said Tabitha with dignity.

"I didn't say that it was. I was just trying to show how time mercifully obliterates. Not what happened but what it felt like."

"We were so *happy* . . ." cried Tabitha. "That's what I can't bear. It was the most perfect feeling I've ever known. And for it all to be wasted."

"It's not wasted. Nothing's wasted. You'll see."

They sat, Tabitha and Zoe, for a minute or so, in silence.

From below in the square came the high continuous sound of children playing; a shaft of evening sunshine came through the window and lay like a topaz flag on the carpet.

Tabitha said, "I'm sorry to be making such a fuss about something so frightfully ordinary."

"If you think it's ordinary," replied Zoe, "then you aren't the girl I think you are. Nor are you feeling what you ought to be feeling."

A small smile glimmered upon Tabitha's face.

"There is nothing ordinary," said Zoe, "about being either happy or unhappy. Whatever the reasons may be. Apart from anything else, I've always assumed that no two people do it in quite the same way."

They faced each other across the room, Tabitha huddled into one end of the sofa, Zoe in the chair. The flag of sunlight climbed up the side of Tabitha's leg and laid one corner on her skirt. Zoe saw in Tabitha's face a whole sequence of other faces, the children that were mother to the woman, while Tabitha heard in Zoe's voice a great many other words, spoken down the years, serious and gay, urgent and inconsequential. Each felt the presence of the other to be bolstered by many other presences and Zoe, suddenly, got up. She crossed the room, poured herself a drink, said to Tabitha, "What about you?"

"O.K. Wine, please."

Zoe sat down again. She began to talk. She talked about Frances and about Steven. She remembered a holiday they had spent in Italy and Christmasses here and there and the time they lost Harry in Piccadilly tube station. The shaft of sunlight died and the room became darker but still warm, as though the day would never really end. And then Zoe said, "I don't know if I'm doing the right thing at the right moment or not, all I know is that it has to be done sooner or later, and maybe too much calculation never did anyone any good. Tab, I'm going to tell you a story . . ."

Tabitha, in amazement, listened.

She let herself into the house and called "Mum . . .?" And even as she said it she realised that the word was not the same as it had been a few hours ago. But, in the event, it had gone unheard. There was a note from Frances on the hall table: "Gone out to dinner. Food for you in the fridge. Don't wait up."

Morris Corfield patrolled his kitchen yet again: table laid, wine opened, saddle of lamb in the oven, fruit salad in the fridge, smoked mackerel for starters laid out on the side. Over the years, he had perfected two menus for entertaining, determined not to become the kind of solitary man who is unable – or professes himself unable – to return hospitality. This was his favourite menu but as he contemplated it he was visited now by doubts. Suppose the lamb was tough? Suppose she didn't care for smoked mackerel? Had he overdone the maraschino in the fruit salad? He returned to the sitting room and stood fretting at the window, alert for the doorbell. Feeling that to invite Frances Brooklyn for the first time on her own might be inappropriate he had provided as ballast another couple and a single man; not knowing how to engineer that these left early, thus allowing him at least a while on his own with her, he had staggered the times at which people were to arrive. Frances was supposed to come at seven thirty, the others at eight. It was now seven thirty-nine, which meant that already things had gone awry.

When, at last, the bell rang he cantered in agitation to the door to find them all there, Frances and the Hadrills in uneasy conjunction on the step, smiling uncertainly at each other, John Peterson approaching down the street. Nothing, he realised gloomily, as he brought them in and settled them, ever goes how it is supposed to go and even as he thought this he met Frances's eye across the room and was smitten with wild irrational happiness. Frances looked immediately away and continued her conversation with John Peterson, and Morris, in his unnerved state, gave the Hadrills each other's drinks and fled to the kitchen in sudden panic about the condition of the roasting lamb. There, he stood for a moment in front of the stove, hot juicy air gusting into his face, and listened to their voices. I feel wonderful, he thought in amazement, whatever is wrong with me? He returned to the sitting room, where the Hadrills were exchanging drinks. He felt as though his emotional state must be apparent to all, like an escaped shirt-tail or unzipped fly.

Half-way through the smoked mackerel John Peterson remarked to Frances, in a correctly subdued tone that referred to her condition, that he had met Steven a couple of times at his university. Morris, anxious to deflect this line, interrupted to explain about John being an academic musicologist. "You've said all that already," put in Susan Hadrill, "When you were giving everybody a run-down on everybody else." Morris glared at her and then, again, caught Frances's eye across the table which looked not disconcerted but amused. He leaned towards her, intensely. "Do you like smoked mackerel?" The enquiry, immediately it was made, seemed suicidal. If she said no, there was nothing to be done.

"I love it."

He sighed. The conversation, thanks to his intrusion, had withered; Morris, ignoring this, got up to pour wine. Frances, he saw had a small mole on the left side of her neck. He sat down again; the smell of the roast lamb was extraordinarily evocative, endowed with significances beyond itself, like incense; he savoured it as though it were none of his doing. The others were talking now. Susan Hadrill said, "Morris, you seem slightly *distrait* tonight. Should I clear the plates?"

And so it went. From the mackerel to the lamb to the fruit salad (the maraschino, in the event, quite satisfactorily adjusted) to the cheeses. Time unfolding and bestowing its own perverse alternatives so that when they rose to move to the sitting room nothing that Morris had planned should be said had been said and it was eleven o'clock. Susan Hadrill, stuffed cosily into the best chair, looked all set for the night. "I always feel bad, Susan," he said sternly, "that you have such miles to come when you visit me. That drive back . . ." And of course it was Frances who glanced at her watch and said, "Goodness, I really must be going."

"Brandy?" said Morris, in a panic, "Whisky? Cointreau? Port . . . um, no, not port."

But people like events are undeflectable. And so when presently the Hadrills and John Peterson arose in concert and announced departure Frances too got up and Morris found himself suddenly in the hall with them all around him, unstoppably heading for the door. She put a hand out for her coat. He said, "Please don't go." She hesitated, the others by now beyond the step. "All right," she said. "Just for a few minutes," and for Morris that heady sense of well-being came rushing back, united now in some permanent way with the smell of roasting lamb. As an afterthought, he waved an effusive farewell to his other guests.

They returned to the sitting room. Where, for a few moments, a potent silence descended.

"Tell me about indexing," said Morris.

"I told you about indexing, at Zoe's party. Didn't I?"

"Yes," said Morris. "I'm afraid I didn't listen properly."

Frances laughed. "You can't really want me to tell you the technicalities of indexing for the second time at . . . at a quarter past midnight. Oughtn't I, by the way, to ring for a taxi?"

"No. I mean no, don't ring for a taxi."

"That was a delicious dinner. You're a very organised cook."

Morris, modestly, ducked his head. "Rather different from our last meal together, though."

"At which I'm afraid I did an awful lot of incoherent talking. I was in a bad state then, as I imagine you realised."

"Yes, I did. You look, if I may say so, much better. But it wasn't incoherent talk. You said things about happiness that I have thought about since."

"Oh dear," said Frances. "I'm afraid I can't remember that bit. I just remember going on about myself rather."

"As a matter of fact," said Morris, "I feel like that tonight. The kind of happiness you were talking about. Those moments one is always going back to, that were perfect. Except that for once it is now, and not then." He looked straight at her, across his sitting room, across the low glass table strewn with books and music magazines, across the balding turkish carpet. He could not imagine why he was being so rash as to say this; he waited in horror for an expression of distaste to come into her eyes.

Frances studied her hands. Then she looked straight at him and said, "I'm so glad. That's a lovely thing to hear someone say."

He breathed again. The implications of what she had said, if there were implications, would have to be investigated later. But he had not wrecked the evening. He beamed.

And Frances saw this puzzling man lit from within, his face – or as much of it as you could see above and behind that neat badgery beard – glowing, his eyes still mild and faintly sad but bright now too. And looking at her in a way that made her feel like another, distant Frances. She too pondered, and discarded for the time being, implications. They sat, for a few moments, in absolute silence; not, this time, so much potent as confused. Morris, washed still with pleasure, could find nothing to say that would not be either banal or a further plunge into hazardous revelations. Frances was seized now with vague alarm and premonitions of melancholy; she knew suddenly that she would wake in the night feeling miserable. She would be obsessed with thoughts of Steven.

They began to talk of their children. On the mantelpiece was a photograph of Morris's son, Mike, as a schoolboy. Frances said, "He lives with his mother?"

"Yes. In Brighton. But he stays with me here often."

"He looks like you."

"So I'm told. Which pleases me. I wonder why that should be – he would be aesthetically better off if he were more like his mother. Very atavistic – the urge to see one's physical self reproduced." And as the words left his mouth he remembered that her children were adopted. He closed his eyes in horror. "I'm sorry."

"Don't be. Yes, it's certainly an instinct I recognise, but I never feel I missed so much. I just needed children. Not having borne them, in the end, mattered less and less, so long as they were there."

Morris nodded, reprieved.

"When Harry was small I used to feel a certain mystery about him. All those physical characteristics of people unknown to me. He has this very straight black hair that must come from someone. And a distinctive nose. Tabitha . . ." She stopped.

"Mike is totally unmysterious," said Morris. He felt that this talk of children had gone far enough; it smacked of middle-age and the side-lines of life and at this moment he felt less middle-aged and more centrally placed than for many a year. He began to talk about a concert series. Frances remarked, with a note of apology, that she was not very musical. "Just so that I don't get myself into a false position."

"But you like to go to a concert occasionally?" said Morris anxiously.

"Oh yes, very much. I just meant that I've never played anything, and I can't read music." She looked at her watch. "You know, Morris, I really should go."

"I'll phone for a taxi."

At the door, he prolonged the departure. The taxi sat throbbing. He had made up his mind to kiss her – after all, social kissing was ubiquitous nowadays, not to do so indeed could be seen as positively dismissive – but when it came to the point he lost his nerve and stood there chuntering on about something until Frances sweetly smiled and turned and was gone.

He went back into the flat and set about the washing up. There was opportunity, now, for analysis of feelings and of what had been said and done. He was amazed at himself. He had not felt like this for such a long time that the experience had the same nostalgic shock as recovery of a taste or smell: peanut butter and childhood, mimosa and his honeymoon in France. He examined his feelings with awe and with apprehension; he searched the evening for what had been right and what had been wrong.

Chapter Thirteen

Tabitha, waking, hung for a moment in that calm anaesthetised world of semi-consciousness in which all was well and then swam up into her gloom as into a chronic illness. She assumed it like a garment and as she did so that insistent something lurking also in the mind took shape, spoke, and last night came pouring back. She lay there and knew that she was a different person from the person she had been yesterday. Across the passage, the phone rang twice in Frances's bedroom; downstairs, the puppy began to bark.

Yesterday she had known one set of things about herself; today, she knew another and consequently nothing could ever be the same again. She thought of a snake she had once seen in the Zoo that had just shed its skin; the old skin lay alongside, a pale abandoned replica. This morning, yesterday's unknowing self seemed to lie beside her.

She got out of bed and went to the mirror. She studied herself and Zoe's eyes looked back at her. She thought of Zoe, and of Frances, and of Steven, and they too were different people, not the people she had known all her life. "I am not going to ask you what you feel about it," Zoe had said, "because you don't know yet. You may not know for some time." But I don't think I am feeling at all, Tabitha thought. What this is like is not so much feeling as being; it is like walking in the wind or sudden blinding heat or that kind of cold that stops you thinking. It is not what I feel but what I am. Simply, I am not who I thought I was, but someone else.

She heard Frances come out of her room and go downstairs. She had a bath and dressed. When she came into the kitchen Frances was at the table, drinking coffee. Tabitha stood there. She said, "Zoe told me."

"I know. She rang just now. She was feeling awful about doing it just like that, without talking to me first. I'm glad, though. We both knew it had to be soon. Here . . ." She poured coffee. "I wish I'd been here when you came in last night."

They faced each other across the table. Frances looked at Tabitha and felt distanced, as though a stranger also sat there. Tabitha looked at Frances and saw someone so familiar that, if required, she could not possibly describe her. She said, "Did you have a nice evening?"

"Did I what? Oh heavens, that . . . Yes, it was fine. Tab . . . I wish I could think of something reasonable to say. Are you all right?"

Tabitha considered. "Actually, I think I'm much more all right than you or Zoe probably expected." Suddenly, she grinned. "Isn't it lucky I've always liked Zoe. I know people who absolutely hate their aunts. Imagine what it would be like then, discovering something like this." She put her elbows on the table, cupped her face in her hands: that small, neat, young face. "Did you know him? The . . . man."

Not, "My father." "No," said Frances.

"Zoe says she has no idea where he is, even. And doesn't want to, unless I do. I don't."

Zoe. Not, "My mother."

"He doesn't seem to come into it, really. Which is odd, I suppose. I don't care about him. Like before I never cared specially about who my parents might have been. Except when I was in a temper with you and Dad."

"You had fantasies sometimes. More than Harry."

"Yes. Even in my wildest fantasies I wouldn't have thought of this."

"No," said Frances, "I daresay not."

"I suppose," Tabitha continued thoughtfully, "there must have been a question of not having me at all. I mean, most people, in that situation, would have had an abortion. She must have thought of that."

"Not for long. For about two and half minutes."

"It's rather odd to think that one might not have been born at all."

"Well," said Frances briskly, "you were. Thank goodness."

"Where did you first see me?"

"In a sort of convent nursing-home place somewhere in France."

A high, shuttered window, stripes of sunlight falling through onto the floor; a street-crier outside; Zoe swamped in huge white pillows, saying, "Give us a kiss. Take her. Quick, take her and go. Before I can think. Take her. She's gorgeous."

"Such ages ago," said Tabitha. "You must almost have forgotten."

"Not all that long ago."

"Do the grandparents know?"

"No. We didn't think they ever should."

Tabitha nodded, apparently in agreement. "Grandma would have had a fit. All much too untidy." She sighed. There were small dark rings under her eyes; she looked suddenly older than twenty-one. Frances, helpless, thought: how old people are depends on what happens to them, not on years.

"Zoe feels guilty," said Tabitha. "She didn't say so, last night, but it kind of leaks out all the time. She must have felt guilty for ever, which is awful. She says she would have made a bloody awful mother. Do you think that's true?"

"I've no idea," said Frances. Unable, now, to look up.

Tabitha sighed again. She rose. "Well, I don't think she needs to feel guilty. I came out of it all rather well, in the end. I mean, I did all right." She touched, for an instant – a quick little dab of the fingers – Frances's hand. "I must do some work. See you later."

Frances, when she had gone, put her head on her arms and cried.

Tabitha, later in the day, telephoned Zoe's office. "I just thought I'd say I'm all right. I mean, I'm not feeling dramatic reactions or anything. In case you were wondering. I daresay you weren't, but just in case."

"I was, as it happens," said Zoe. "Well, good."

"It's difficult to work, that's the only thing. But that's been difficult for weeks."

"Then chuck it. Go and do something fun."

"I talked to Mum."

"Ah."

" 'Bye, then. See you."

"See you, love," said Zoe.

Tabitha stowed her books tidily at the back of her desk and, again, went out into London. For quite long periods, during the last twenty-four hours, she realised, she had not thought of him. She wondered if perhaps she might be on the mend, but when the bus passed Great Russell Street the mourning returned. She saw that other unreachable Tabitha, forever crossing the street with her hand in his, in a glass bubble of happiness, while she, the real Tabitha, was swept away and onwards like a swimmer amid unrelenting tides. She wondered, if this was how it was, how people got through life, always yearning backwards, picking up the afterglow of other times like the heat that lingers in a stone wall at the end of a sunny day. How do people carry all this around, without being dragged down? It seemed extraordinary that she and they should look out onto the same streets and buildings, locked each into private visions.

She went to Trafalgar Square. She wandered for a while among the crowds and then into the National Portrait Gallery. She walked from picture to picture; she looked into the dead varnished eyes and thought about feelings, about grief and joy. Admittedly, these were the famous, but the famous presumably have feelings like anyone else. Charlotte Brönte was in love. Charles the First must have known about fear. There is religious fervour and fanaticism and greed. People look outwards from portraits as though it were they who were the spectators; they look over your shoulder at some invisible display. Ranged in the cool creaking rooms of a gallery it is they who are permanent, not those who pass before them.

Tabitha sat down in front of an eighteenth century grandee with whose name she was unfamiliar and tugged at the strap of her sandal, which was making her foot hurt. The man in the picture had lived from seventeen twenty until seventeen eighty-five and indeed his face was so firmly of that time that there was no need for the little gold plaque, though whether this was due to a style of painting or to some curious chronological conditioning it would be impossible to say. Her own face, swimming above his in the reflection on the glass, seemed equally firmly of today. Its kindred looked at her from advertisements and off the television screen – girls who of course were not the same but bore a family resemblance. Everything about you, she thought, ties you up to something else: parents, the time in which you live. Who you are is where you come from. And all the while we leave ourselves behind reflected in their gilt frames. Like I am left behind in Great Russell Street and on that hillside in Scotland and here on this seat, bending down to fix the sandal strap so it won't rub.

Zoe crammed papers into a briefcase, rummaged in her bag for glasses, keys, cheque book, let herself out of the flat, raced down the stairs. In the taxi she subsided. When in my life, she thought, have I ever started the day except like a bullet from a gun? Ah well, tranquillity was never for me. She got out her diary, scribbled on a page already clotted with entries, opened a newspaper. But, as the taxi sat at a traffic light, the paper dropped from her hands and she stared at a woman on the pavement, a woman holding the hand of a small girl. The child, for an instant, had

Tabitha's face: Tabitha's face in another summer, an eight year old face, warily looking out from behind a screen of dark hair. The woman and the child crossed the road, holding hands, and Zoe continued to watch them until the lights changed. I don't deserve it, she thought, I don't deserve it that she should have taken it as she has. She could have hated me, she would have been entitled. Instead of which she sits there with her grave odd face, taking it all in, making God knows what colossal adjustments.

And Zoe was filled, all of a sudden, with pleasure. Life is not too bad, she thought, in fact come to that life is pretty damn good. She rode through the city, intent upon this inner well being, and when at last the taxi stopped she continued to sit until the driver craned round to say "Barts. The hospital. You said Barts, didn't you?"

Re-dressing, she could hear the doctor washing his hands beyond the curtain. When she came through he was sitting at his desk, writing. "And this has been going on for several months, Miss Brooklyn?"

"Yes."

"You should have come before."

How they do like to rap you over the knuckles, these people, Zoe thought. "If you turn a blind eye to a problem there's always a good chance it'll lose its nerve," she said cheerfully. And I never could be bothered fussing over the blights of femininity. Certainly I'm not going to waste time over some damn menopausal ailment. She glanced at her watch. You kept me waiting fifty minutes, chum, my time costs money too. "O.K." – placatingly – "I should have come. Sorry."

The doctor, now, was consulting a list. He looked at her. He began to talk. And Zoe, listening, registering with shock and amazement what he was saying, found herself studying his face, an unfamiliar face, a somewhat unappealing face. How perverse, she thought, that some of the more intense moments of one's life should take place in intimacy with people one does not know. She saw, quite clearly, the long-since face of a French nun leaning over her, holding a mewing baby. The doctor finished what he had to say and waited for her to speak; she could think only that his face, too, would loiter in the head.

She said to Frances, "Oh, by the way – I'll be away for a few days from the end of next week. A job in Rome. So don't bother to ring."

Through the ensuing days she smiled. She smiled at people and talked of other things and within she felt the queasy hollowness of fear. And a great solitude. She lay awake at night, reading to pass the hours. But her eyes travelled over the print and she talked to herself. She said: It is not necessarily cancer. From what he said I would make an informed guess that there is about a fifty per cent chance that it is not. Which means that there is a fifty per cent chance that it is. And if it is, as he so delicately explained, there is a good deal that can be done. "One of the more treatable ones." Well, this time next week I shall know. I shall come out of the anaesthetic and someone in a white gown will sit by the bed and tell me, in good B movie style.

She was suffused with rage. The rage, at times, drove out the fear and she hurried about what she had to do in a storm of indignation. I haven't time to be ill, she fumed, I have too darn much to do, above all I haven't time to die.

The world had never shone so brightly. Wherever she went in the city she was transfixed, as though she saw for the first time the crisp frontages of the Nash terraces, the symmetries of the darkly stooping trees in the parks, the opalescence of clouds above the river. She watched from her window, from buses and taxis, and recorded its indifference. She could not decide if the inhumanity of what she saw outweighed its pleasure; she worried at this as though there might be a correct answer. Is the physical world a comfort or not?

When Tabitha telephoned Zoe was brisk and gay. Tabitha would be going back to Cambridge next week. "I have to go away for a few days," said Zoe. "See you thereafter . . ."

She could not endure sympathy. The rest she could stand, would get through with. Alone. If I have to come to it, she thought, the visits and the forced optimism and the bloody flowers and the damn grapes, then I have to come to it. But for the time being I'll do it on my own.

There is time, which is supposed to be linear, and there are seconds and minutes and hours which are supposed to be of a particular duration. And there are also days, in which we live. The day on which Zoe went into hospital was not linear, neither was it composed of minutes or hours that bore any resemblance to one another. They raced, or they crept. Occasionally the day stopped altogether and hung suspended in the greenish light of the ward, quite self-contained, like the sterile world of a space capsule.

Once, obediently, Zoe padded down corridors in her dressing-gown and slippers to be wired up to a machine that whirred and clicked and showered figures and numbers across a television screen. "Your heart," said a woman in white, "is quite normal."

"I'm glad to hear it," replied Zoe. "I've sometimes wondered." The woman smiled. "Back to the ward now. Can you find your way?" Zoe padded off, past ordinary people in their suits and dresses and jackets, a creature apart. Now I know, she thought, why the first thing they do with prisoners is remove their clothes.

In the ward, she sat on a chair reading. Nurses, from time to time, tried to tidy her away into the bed. "No thanks," said Zoe. "If you don't mind. I'm not ill till tomorrow."

Most of the women were old. Their grey or white hair was a curious affront to their pastel nightclothes, to the lemon nylon and pale pink candlewick and the frills and arch transparencies, as though they were macabre dolls. Some sat propped against pillows, others shuffled past, peeping at Zoe with curious eyes. She was offered sweets and newspapers; hospitals are kindly places; people are nice to one another. Sometimes it was still morning, the morning on which she had been told to present herself, and at other times a gilded evening light flooded down through the high windows, striping the shiny linoleum floor. The day folded back and forth; she was no longer in real time, just as she was no longer in the real world.

She tried to penetrate the customs of the place, as though it were an alien society; nurses, she noted, are labelled by name and their rank denoted by subtleties of dress. She observed caps and the colours of sleeves. She talked to a young woman hooked up to a Christmas tree of chrome and tubes and bright pouches of blood and serum. "What are you in for?" asked the girl. "Armed robbery," said Zoe. The girl, clutching her side, laughed, and the Christmas tree danced and glinted. An old woman shuffled by on her way to the lavatory, steered from behind by a nurse with both hands on her hips; the light shone through the old woman's nightdress so that her body beneath was like a statue, heavy thighs and sagging breasts, a dark clump of pubic hair.

A young woman doctor came and talked to Zoe. "Don't worry," she kept saying. "I'm not," said Zoe with honesty. What she felt was not worry but a curious deadening, akin to hopelessness; she had stepped aside from life, and did not expect to step back.

In the evening, she got into the bed. The ward doors were opened and visitors arrived, homing upon the bedsides to sit awkwardly there like gaolers or ministering priests. When the bell rang and they left the ward seemed to heave a little with relief. Nurses came round with trolleys, dishing out pills and drug cocktails in tiny plastic cups. Zoe was given a mug of ovaltine and a sleeping pill. "Nothing more for you till after the op," said the nurse. "They'll be taking you down to the theatre at ten." Zoe declined the pill. "Sure?" said the nurse doubtfully. "Some people feel a bit wakeful, the night before." "No thanks," said Zoe. "I've never touched the things."

She did not sleep at all. Time had failed altogether. Now and for always she lay in the twilight of the ward, listening sometimes to the noises – the squeak of the nurses' shoes, the sighs and moans of patients – and drifting at other times into a kind of privacy in which she summoned up ghosts. She talked to Steven and to Frances. She shuffled the pack of days and selected one here and one there; she lay with Eric in a bed in Prague, when first she knew him; she watched an infant Tabitha take her first wobbling steps across a sun-blotched lawn; she had a row with a one-time boss, a glorious liberating eruptive moment of verbal violence, as cleansing to the spirit as absolution. But for the most part she simply lay there, passive, alone and yet surrounded by people whose breathings and sighings gave to the ward a corporate life as though it were some great somnolent creature. From time to time there were crises: someone would call out, nurses pattered to and fro. Screens were put round a bed; a doctor came. Beyond the screens voices muttered. A nurse kept saying, "It's all right, dear." Someone groaned and groaned. Zoe turned on to her side. When it was daylight the screens were gone and the bed was empty, clean sheets strapped tightly to the mattress. She thought, I have been present at the death of a person I never knew.

It was another day. Early morning of another day. The end of which was invisible in a particular sense. All days are open-ended, she thought, this one is more open than others. And with the thought came an odd tranquillity. The dull queasiness that had gnawed at her for a week now ebbed away and in its place there came a determination. She knew that whichever way it turned out, she had gained something in these last surreal hours. She remembered what she herself had said to Tabitha: Nothing is wasted.

The woman doctor returned. She said, "All right?" She sat for a moment on Zoe's bed; her young face was strained with fatigue. Zoe said, "I'm fine, love." She added, "You've been up half the night, haven't you?" The girl nodded. This place is driving me sentimental, Zoe thought, something is happening to my natural distrust of humanity. I keep seeing goodness.

She was given an injection, and floated into a careless drunken world in which nothing really mattered. An elderly Pakistani toured the ward with an immense floor-polisher, importantly poking it beneath the beds. He said to Zoe, "Machine is coming."

"So I see," said Zoe. "Is very good machine, is doing very good cleaning"; the hospital and its mysterious workings were relegated, he ran his hand down the metal stem of the polisher with respectful familiarity, like a groom handling a thoroughbred. "It's a beautiful machine," said Zoe.

Presently, hands lifted her on to a trolley. She slid down corridors, gazing at the shiny ceilings. Time ceased altogether.

Morris and Frances sat in deck chairs in Green Park. At a short distance the band played, bestowing an atmosphere of decorous carnival. Dogs scampered; a child turned somersaults; Frances said, "What a good idea this was." Morris glowed.

It was their second outing. She had come with him to a South Bank concert and now, a week later, he had felt able to telephone at short notice and wonder if she would care for an afternoon at Burlington House, followed by tea in the park. And here they were. From time to time Morris gazed, furtively, at Frances. She wore a sea-green dress and high-heeled sandals. He liked the way she wore very little make-up and the streak of grey across the front of her fair hair was undisguised; deceptions, of any kind, had always irritated him. A tribulation of his professional life was the interviewing of opera divas that he from time to time had to do. One glossy lady had lied so prodigiously about her age that he had listened to her with distaste ever since. Which was irrational: her voice remained the same. Preoccupied, momentarily, with this theme of honesty, it occurred to him that there was one thing he ought to make clear before this friendship, if friendship it were to be, got any further. He said, "My wife left me."

"Yes," said Frances. "You said so. When we met in Venice."

Morris, doggedly, added, "I mean she simply got tired of me. It wasn't that there was anyone else." It occurred to him, now, that he might be inflicting confidences where they were not welcome. In confusion, he added, "Not that it matters."

"Of course it matters," said Frances. "It must have been awful. But it's all over now, I imagine."

"In so far as things are ever over."

"That's a gloomy line to take. And quite the wrong one for me just now."

"I'm sorry," said Morris, in anguish. "That was thoughtless." After a moment he went on tentatively, "Are things . . . any better?"

"Sometimes they're better and sometimes they're not. But probably more better than worse." Frances paused; the band finished a selection from *The Mikado* and there was a flutter of applause. "I got absurdly distressed a couple of weeks ago because I found that Steven had been briefly engaged to someone before I met him. It unnerved me, in some way, that that should always have existed and I never knew. But I think I've digested it now. It doesn't seem so important."

Morris nodded. He wished that he had not asked that. Now the husband hung there again, an inhibiting presence. I must not get into the position of some kind of therapist, he thought, that would be to start off on the wrong foot. He pushed Steven aside, with a twinge of guilt. "I've been putting into practice your advice about indexing. The thing begins to look more shapely."

"Good," said Frances. And beamed. "It's nice to be useful."

At which point Morris became, it later seemed to him, slightly unhinged. He reached out across the gap between their two chairs and took her hand. They sat there, thus, looking at one another. Frances wore an expression of mild panic which Morris misinterpreted as distaste; he continued to hold her hand but his stomach lurched and he could find nothing to say. Frances, in anxiety, could only think: But you are not Steven; I don't know if I can go on with this; you are not Steven.

Tabitha, on the train to Cambridge, watched the landscape flow past; the same landscape that had flown the other way three months before. Opposite, a young man she slightly knew, a medical student, was going on about dissection. "Yuck," said Tabitha, "I don't know how you can." A small town streamed by: church tower, wet slate roofs, red brick cartwheels of a housing estate; I've seen that before, she thought, I remember the church. "Is it right," she said, "that your blood cells are changing all the time?"

"They renew themselves," said the medical student, "every few weeks."

"And skin?"

"That's growing and flaking all the time."

"I am not physically the same person that I was three months ago," said Tabitha. "Not even that."

"Oh well, come on," said the boy. "Bones . . . Muscles . . . Do you want a cup of coffee?"

"Thanks," said Tabitha. The boy went off to the buffet car and she continued to watch the landscape. It is much more than three months, she thought, since I came past here; time is not only to do with months or weeks, it is to do with feelings and what you know and who you are. Time eats you up; there is practically nothing of me that is the same when I last saw that church, those trees.

Chapter Fourteen

When Zoe came swimming up into the world again the figure beside her bed was not white-gowned but dressed in blue and was smiling. The ward sister said, "There you are, back with us."

Zoe gazed at this face which she had known for twenty-four hours and which seemed more familiar to her than any she had ever known.

"You're fine. No malignancy. They had to do a hysterectomy so you're going to be feeling a bit sore."

"That's all right," said Zoe, "I have all the children I want."

"Well, good," said the woman briskly. "And now why don't you have a little sleep. You've nothing to worry about any more."

It was early afternoon. The ward still had that greenish underwater atmosphere, but from somewhere outside there came a murmur of traffic. Feet tapped along a pavement; someone was whistling. Zoe lay quite still. The way she felt reminded her of something and somehow the most immediate thing was to remember what. And then it came to her. In just such a state of transcendental joy had one lain as a very small girl with the knowledge that unseen but quite tangible the Christmas stocking rested plumply against the end of the bed. She laughed, out loud. The woman next to her peered round a magazine, startled. "It's all right," said Zoe, "I just thought of something ridiculous."

She closed her eyes. If one were religious, she thought, there would be something positive to be done. Prayers of thanksgiving. Candles. Gifts to charity. Implementation of all those vows of virtue if spared. For the agnostic *hoi polloi* there is nothing. Nothing but this amazing sense of being the object of a miracle. That the thunderbolt has fallen elsewhere, again.

She began to drift into sleep. But even as she did so she knew, quite clearly, that despite all that nothing would ever be quite as it was. Even with no-one to be grateful to, the emotion remained. I feel shriven, she thought, I am not the same as I was yesterday, or any of my yesterdays.

Frances, in those early weeks and months of her grief, had found ritual examinations of her state of mind mildly therapeutic. They had not helped much, but they had helped a little. Daily, she had assessed herself; whether she felt worse than the day before, or not. She seized on the occasional tranquil hour as a trophy, entered it on the chart. She logged unflinchingly the days of deterioration. Out of it, something might come.

Now, on a morning in early October, she came downstairs through her house and was pleased with what she saw. She drew back the curtains in the sitting room and early sun flooded in. She opened the french window and stepped out into the small garden. She had cleared and re-planted the beds herself; paving had been laid to make a small terrace, new creepers reached tentatively up the wall of the house. Today she would fill the tubs with bulbs for the spring. Next summer, she would sit out here; a bench must be bought, a table . . .

She went back through the house into the kitchen. In the sitting room, she tidied a heap of books dumped on the table by Harry last night, plumped up cushions. The photographs on the book-case had been pushed aside by a pile of newspapers; she removed the papers and straightened the photographs: Steven, the children. As she did so she realised that she was performing these small tasks not out of duty but with pleasure. She inhabited, now, this house; it gave her satisfaction to arrange its rooms, to dispose around them the things she had kept from the other house, to add a few more – new curtains, a rug.

In the hall ticked the long-case clock that had been a wedding present from her parents. Steven's desk stood in the sitting room. On the kitchen dresser hung the quirkily-shaped pottery mug made by Tabitha in the school art class. And while these objects had still the power to cause pain, to make her eyes prick at moments of vulnerability, they had taken on also the quality of anchors. Sometimes, she was uncertain which was stronger – their capacity to distress or to reassure. But she knew that she could not do without them.

She went through into the kitchen and began to get breakfast. Harry had arrived back a few days before; he had spent most of the time since asleep, like the survivor of some military campaign. Now, she could hear him moving around overhead and presently he came down. He stood in the doorway, blinking.

"Where's Tab these days?"

"Harry! I told you – she went back to Cambridge."

"Oh yes, sure. I forgot."

"I'm glad you've surfaced. You'd better come with me to see the grandmothers today. It's the last chance before you go. I'm working the rest of this week."

"Will do . . ." He poured himself a cup of coffee. "Is it O.K., this job?"

"It's all right. In fact I quite enjoy it. I am about to be briefed in the use of some alarming new piece of office machinery. A sort of computer thing."

"Ah," said Harry. "No problem," he went on, dismissively. "Can I do a fry-up?"

"Yes. Well, electronics have never been my strong point. Let's hope I manage to come out on top."

"No problem," repeated Harry, unfurling strips of bacon into the pan. He stood at the stove, frowning slightly as though perturbed by what she had just said. In fact, as Frances guessed, he was thinking of something quite different and, indeed, began in a moment to discuss a logistical problem to do with the transport of his possessions to college later in the week. The self-absorption of the young, she thought with resentful indulgence, is like a perpetual heavy cold, locking out much that goes on beyond the sufferer's head. She watched him, covertly; the dent in the back of his neck that was for some reason so intensely moving in small boys and that even now, in maturity, evoked feelings of tenderness; the vaguely oriental caste to his features that implied confused and mysterious ancestries; the familiar but now gatheringly strange Harry-ness of him. In a year or two, he would be someone quite different; a relative only of the child she had raised.

She said, "Harry, there's something I've got to tell you. Now's as good a time as ever. It's about Tab."

He sat there, eating bacon and eggs, listening, placing eventually his knife and fork neatly together on his plate, looking not at her but steadily at the table.

When she had finished he said, "Is that all?"

"All?" Frances, shaken, stared at him.

"I mean. It's just Tab?"

"Oh, heavens, yes. Not you. No revelations about you. Everything's just as it always was."

Harry wiped his mouth. "Simply that one likes to know where one is." He sounded brusque; in fact, as Frances recognised, was assuming the false nonchalance of one glimpsing undreamed-of complexities. After a moment he added, with deliberate casualness, "How does Tab feel about it?"

"It was a bit of a shock, I'm afraid."

"Actually," said Harry, "Tab looks rather like Zoe. It had never occurred to me before."

"Yes."

They sat in silence. The puppy, under the table, whimpered, like a child sensing tension. Harry said, "Do you like it?"

"Like what?"

"The dog."

"Oh," said Frances. "Him. Yes, of course I do. I've got very fond of him. I've called him Hector, by the way. I needed a name to shout – you know, when he gets out into the street."

"Why Hector?"

"Because I happened to be putting Dad's *Companion to Classical Literature* in the new bookshelves when I was thinking about a name."

Harry frowned. "Actually I'd have thought it was a bit much, for a puppy."

"I did wonder," said Frances apologetically.

"Oh well. I expect it'll be all right later on."

There was a pause. Harry, through a mouthful of richly buttered toast, enquired after Zoe.

"She's fine. In Rome just now, I think."

"I daresay I'll see her before I go. Do I," he added, "have to say anything about . . . this?"

"Not unless you want to."

Harry considered. "I think I won't actually." He rose. "I'm off now. I'm meeting Nick. See you."

The subject, she realised, was closed. For now and possibly for ever. And I don't know, she thought, what he feels and thinks about it, if anything, and probably never will. Is he embarrassed? Does he feel excluded? Or is it, simply, a fact that he has digested, like he digested being blown up at Venice airport? Perhaps he is one of those people who are able to go through life step by step, for whom what happens, happens, and that is that. For whom today is uncontaminated by yesterday.

The doorbell rang. Marsha Landon was on the step, standing with her back to the door as though about to depart. Frances's spirits slumped instantly at the sight of her; only the week before she had successfully avoided Philip in the local supermarket.

Marsha turned round. "I thought you must be out." She sounded aggrieved, almost accusing.

"I probably didn't hear the bell the first time." Marsha, Frances now saw, had a plum-coloured weal across her cheekbone. "Oh dear, you've had an accident."

"No," Marsha walked into the hall. "Philip did it."

I don't want to know about this, Frances thought. I simply do not want to know.

"Last night."

They went into the kitchen.

"He was pissed, of course," said Marsha. "Not that that makes any difference."

Frances put the kettle on, in silence.

"I've been to the doctor. I told him I walked into a door, but I don't imagine he was fooled. He said it's just a bad bruise, it'll go down, there's nothing broken." She touched her face, self-consciously; the gesture reminded Frances of children brandishing minor injuries. "He's gone off somewhere now. He always does after something like this. He'll be back."

Frances put the mugs of coffee on the table, and pushed a plate of biscuits towards Marsha.

"No, thanks. I've just had breakfast. I went round to Chris early, I had to have someone to talk to."

"I see."

"But she had to go to work, so . . . I mean it's not that I'm in a terrible state or anything. All this has happened often enough before, for Christ's sake. Just one needs to be with someone, know what I mean . . ."

"Marsha," said Frances. "Why don't you leave Philip?"

Marsha stared. "Leave him?"

"If it's all so awful."

Marsha shrugged. After a moment she said, "I'd be alone, wouldn't I?"

"And would that be so much worse?"

"Well . . ." Marsha's look, across the mug of coffee, was almost shifty, "I suppose he's better than nothing."

Frances said sharply, (surprised at her own tone, as though she heard someone else speaking) "If you find living with a man who apparently has made you unhappy for years preferable to living alone, then you have a problem which is quite over and beyond your problems with Philip."

"You're alone, and I don't imagine . . ."

"Please don't try to imagine anything about me. I am alone, yes, and I think I prefer my condition to yours." Frances got up. She took the empty mugs over to the sink and rinsed them out. She dried them and put them back on the hooks. She turned to Marsha, "Look, I'm sorry you've had this row, or whatever it was. But I'm not at all sure what help I can be. I don't think sitting around picking it over does anyone much good. If I were you I'd get on and do something. Clean your house up. Anything. And I've got to go out, I'm afraid."

Marsha said, with a trace of resentment, "You're an awfully *positive* person, Frances. I just couldn't be like that. I'd better go anyway. There's no food in the house. God, how I loathe shopping."

At the front door she paused. "Actually, Philip might very well turn up here. He tends to go looking for shoulders to weep on. And he fancies you, I could tell. I don't mind – don't think that. Actually things are often rather better when he's . . . well, sort of got someone. If you and he are friendly it's quite all right by me, in fact it might . . ."

Frances, sharply interrupting, said, "I've not seen him for several weeks. I'm busy these days. I have a job."

Marsha gazed. "Oh, I see. Well, 'bye then."

When she had gone Frances felt guilty. I was cruel, she told herself. All right, she is stupid and parasitic and hopeless, but I had no right to be as I was. Uncharitable. There, but for the grace of God or someone or something, go I. She is not, of course, correct in saying that I am a positive person, whatever that may mean. Simply, I have known what it is to be happy and she poor creature probably never has. Even what has gone is sustenance, to have been happy once is a privilege. I am not damned but blessed.

Zoe, coming into the press conference, saw Eric at the far side of the room and beside him the girl, her, she who was now presumably his wife. O.K., she thought, this is it. This was coming, sooner or later. Let's take it now, sooner rather than later, and get it over with.

She crossed the room. "Hi, there!"

The girl – the wife, she – jumped and flushed and collected herself and gabbled greetings that were a shade too warm. Eric said, "Zoe. Hello. How are you?"

"I am fine," said Zoe. She beamed (noting that amazingly to do so was not so hard after all). "As it happens it's rather good to be able to say that. I'm fine."

"You're looking," said the girl, (the wife, her) "awfully well."

"And so," said Zoe, "are you. The both of you." Beaming still (and noting also that while of course one's natural expression is and ever has been remorselessly cheerful, all the same one was doing really rather well).

"Frances?" enquired Eric. "Tabitha? Harry?" Squirming in his chair, looking if ever a man did in manifest discomfort and wishing himself a hundred miles away.

"Fine," said Zoe. "All fine." Adding, silently: And calm down, love, cool it, this is something we both have to go through. And come on, it was worth it, wasn't it? All those times, good, bad and indifferent. Mostly good. All that love and warmth and yes, anger occasionally. Of course it was worth it.

She looked down at them, and the faces that had had such potency when she came into the room – such power to make the stomach churn and the heart thump – became all of a sudden mundane. Eric's was, simply, familiar: a face known for time out of mind and with, yes, certain emotive force, now and forever. The girl's – hers – was just a face, satisfactorily constructed, pretty indeed (the nose a trifle lumpy, maybe . . .).

"Well," she said. "To our muttons, I suppose. Here come the boys. See you around, I don't doubt."

And, sitting down, opening her notepad, observing that the politician on display had put on weight and wore a deplorable tie, she thought: There, that wasn't too bad, was it? We are through that and out the other side and whatever I am feeling is endurable. I have had my mind wonderfully concentrated, this last couple of weeks. I know for what we should give thanks. To be sitting here, in good health and reasonably good spirits listening to this fellow who is still wet behind the ears explain how he will restore this country to wealth, prosperity and international prestige.

Each morning when Morris woke he knew before conscious thought arrived that there was something enormously beneficial in progress, some matter for exultation. That to be entering the day was good. Pleasure loitered somewhere just out of sight. And then as he woke up properly he remembered.

If there was no arrangement to see her, then he could always anticipate telephoning her. He could think: this afternoon I shall hear her voice, tomorrow, the next day . . . On the other hand if there was an arrangement on the horizon he could savour it: on Friday we shall go to the concert together, at the weekend I am to go to the house, the day after tomorrow I shall see her. Expectation was almost as sweet as reality; it lasted longer, for one thing.

When he passed young couples in the street walking hand in hand he felt conspiratorial sympathy; he wanted to pat them on the shoulder and say, you may not believe this, looking at me, middle-aged and all that, but I know how you feel. Me too. He could hardly believe his luck. Unless you were some kind of emotional profligate, he supposed, the chances of running up against the appropriate person three times in one's life were slim. You met, after all, hundreds of people; nearly all were the wrong age, the wrong sex, wrongly disposed towards you or simply not to your taste. He had now fallen in love three times. The first time had been with a girl at college and had been an education of the senses in every way, but impermanent. The second had been with his ex-wife and while that too had proved ultimately impermanent and indeed the basis of much misery, the distant flavour of those early months lingered yet. And now there was this, out of which goodness knows what would come. He dared not dwell on that. For one thing, he was still deeply uncertain how she felt about him; she seemed to enjoy herself when they were together; she looked at him, he thought, with affection. But he was not sure.

He was filled with what he felt to be prurient curiosity about Steven. Despising himself, he went to a library and looked up his books; the man had apparently been inordinately clever. And good-looking too: from a back flap stared (assessing, perceiving . . .) one of those spectacled and indubitably intellectual but also virile faces: an academic Arthur Miller. Morris, with a mixture of respect and resentment, stared back. He told himself that there was nothing so irrational or indeed downright tasteless as to feel jealous of a man who was dead, but jealous was what he felt. Steven's inaccessible presence filled up the whole of Frances's past; everything to which she referred implied him, in some way or another. I am going to have to come to terms with him, thought Morris, if we are to get anywhere at all. He bought a paperback edition of Steven's book on disarmament and read it carefully, several times disagreeing with an argument which gave him a perverse satisfaction.

Frances, for her part, tended to waken into a state of perplexity. She would perform the ritual examination of her condition and find, day by day, that it was not too bad. She would think of Steven, testing herself. Sometimes that was endurable and at others it was not. She would think about what she was planning to do that day. And then, probably she would think of Morris and a certain confusion would ensue. She liked him; she was uncomfortably aware of what he felt about her; her own response was bewilderingly complex.

When as on that occasion in the park, he touched her, she shrank with alarm; a part of her rejoiced and responded, another part retreated in horror. And at the same time she saw the look in his eyes, and was filled with distress.

The third occasion on which Morris came to see her at the house was the anniversary of Steven's death. She had confronted this with resolution, treating it as any other day, making no special plans, but when Morris rang, unexpectedly, to ask if he might drop in for an hour or two on his way to a concert, she had been inordinately relieved, though she did not tell him so. She realised that she had dreaded being alone all day.

It was a fine warm evening. They sat on the newly arranged terrace, amid the tubs planted with bulbs and the young climbing plants. The puppy sat at their feet, chewing a rubber bone that Harry had bought for it. Behind them, the french windows were open to the house. Frances thought: A year ago none of this was known to me: this place, this man, this version of myself. She felt suddenly disoriented and looked away. Morris was talking about Aldeburgh. He broke off: "I'm sorry. I mustn't forever go on about music."

Frances smiled. "You don't. It comes up most discreetly. And I inflict shop on you. I talk about the office."

"How is this new machinery you have to use?"

She gazed blankly. "Machinery?"

"This computer or whatever."

"Oh – that. A bit daunting, but I think I have the upper hand."

Morris said solicitously, "Are you all right?"

"I'm fine. Sorry. I'm being a bit vague tonight, I'm afraid."

"Vague is all right. I was just afraid there might be something wrong."

"Nothing wrong at all."

They viewed each other across Frances's new slatted wooden garden table. Morris, hesitating on the brink of several crucial openings, was silent. Frances, taking herself in hand, thought: this is where I am now, this is where I live, this is the person that I am and it is not all bad, not bad at all. Everything else is over and gone, with all that that means. The puppy got up and went into the house.

She said, "Are we warm enough out here?"

"I'm quite warm enough."

"Then so am I." And indeed, the sunlight on her arm was like a hand laid on the skin.

"For me," said Morris, "autumn always feels like the beginning of the year. Things starting up. An urban attitude, I know. Concerts, theatres."

"Steven used to say that too. For him of course it was being hitched to the academic cycle."

"Of course," said Morris, in a rather flat tone and Frances thought, why did I say that? Why even when I am most determined not to am I looking over my shoulder for Steven?

A small wind had got up. Somewhere inside the house a door banged. Frances said, "Maybe we will go in. Anyway, I want to show you my reorganisations. I have made myself a study. The first I have ever had."

"And what," said Morris cheerfully, "will you study?" He followed her into the sitting room.

A few minutes later, when they had toured the house to inspect the changes, Frances realised that the puppy was missing. "It must have got out. I must have left the front door open – that was what that bang was. Bother. Morris, I'm sorry – I shall have to go and look for him."

They walked down the street together, searching. "Does he know where he lives?" asked Morris. Frances said, "I've no idea. Animals are supposed to have a homing instinct, aren't they? He's my first dog, remember. And last, too, if this kind of thing is going to go on."

When they saw him he was nosing at a dustbin. Frances called; he caught sight of them at the same moment and came bounding up the street. The car that hit him came out of a side turning and could not have avoided him. It flung him up into the air with a curious slow motion effect so that for weeks afterwards both Morris and Frances carried in their heads the sight of that limp brown body turning over and over to flop down on the pavement like a sack.

It was Morris who examined him. He said, "I'm afraid he's dead." The driver of the car, a middle-aged West Indian, was making noises of regret and apology. Frances said, "You're not to blame. You couldn't help it. Please don't bother to stay. We'll have to take him back to the house," she went on, to Morris, "I'd better . . ." The West Indian dived into the back of his car and emerged with a Woolworths plastic carrier bag. He held it out to Morris who hesitated and then took it. "Thank you." He put the body of the dog into the carrier bag and turned to Frances. She had gone quite white, he saw. He took her arm and they walked thus back to the house, the plastic bag bumping awkwardly against Morris's leg.

When they were in the hall Frances said, "The stupid thing was to call him. It was my fault."

"It wasn't anyone's fault. It simply happened." Morris carried the bag through on to the terrace and put it down beside the window. Frances went into the sitting room and sat down. After five minutes he joined her. "I've rung the local council. They'll send a van along to take him away."

Frances said, "I'd never have thought of that. I wouldn't have known what to do."

"A friend of mine had a business with a cat once." He s down beside her on the sofa.

"Damn," said Frances. "I'm afraid I'm weeping." She got out a kleenex and blew her nose. Tears, Morris saw, were coursing down her cheeks. It occurred to him that he had not seen anyone cry for years. Very many years. Not since the end of his marriage and his wife had not in fact been a woman who often wept. He felt not in the least embarrassed but almost unendurably tender. He said, "I'll get you another dog."

"I don't want another. I didn't really want this one. But thank you, Morris. It's not to do with the dog at all. Though I did like him."

"I know it's not to do with the dog."

"Small things tend to unnerve me. It's tiresome."

"It wasn't all that small a thing."

"No. Poor Hector. I don't think he knew much about it."

Morris got up. "I think it might be a good thing if we both had a drink, don't you? Let me get them."

When he returned Frances had restored herself. Her face was dry and her hair combed. She took the drink. "Thank you. I'm lucky you were here. It would have been much worse otherwise."

"If I hadn't been here it probably wouldn't have happened. You opened the front door for me and then, apparently, left it open."

"Now who's appropriating blame?"

"No," said Morris. "I'm just saying that there are innumerable alternative pasts. Everything might always not have happened. But it did. So what happens next remorselessly ensues. Once Susanna has revealed the Count's intentions to Figaro the rest of the Marriage must unfold as it does."

Frances sat up abruptly. "Morris . . . your concert. Surely you should have gone ages ago?"

"I'm not going to get to the concert," said Morris. "And I don't particularly care I'm afraid."

And when, a few minutes later, he kissed her, it occurred to him, even in the middle of that delightful and unbelievable process that when he got up that morning this had been lying in wait for him at the end of the day, undreamed-of but inevitable.

He said, "Oh, Frances, I do so very much want you."

And Frances, shaking slightly, looked at him and could think only how strange it was that behind this face, seen now more intensely than before, there lay no other. The faces of Tabitha, Zoe, Harry, of friends, were palimpsests: behind them lurked others, their younger selves, they were continuous, as she was herself. Morris was as he was and could not be otherwise: his neat triangular beard slightly flecked with grey, his sharp brown eyes, the little pouches beneath them.

He drew away from her. He finished his drink and said, "I don't mean now this minute. It would be all wrong tonight, when you've been upset. But sometime, I do so hope. And now I think we should go out and have a meal somewhere, don't you?"

Chapter Fifteen

"I have this pompous card," said Zoe, "with gilt crawling all over it, inviting me to the first Steven Brooklyn Memorial Lecture. We go, I suppose."

Frances said, "I suppose."

Zoe looked at her intently. "You don't absolutely have to."

"Of course I shall go."

Zoe prowled the room. "I must say, this place is a treat now. Much better than that mausoleum." She pounced at the mantelpiece. "I haven't seen that before."

"Morris Corfield gave it to me," said Frances, over-casually. "When the puppy was killed. As a sort of joke, I think."

Zoe peered. "Nice expensive joke, early Victorian stuff like that. It looks like Herring or someone. I like the schmaltzy dog. He's a real nice guy, Morris, isn't he?"

"Yes."

"Ho, hum," said Zoe. "Ah well. Nuff said, I daresay. Tab

rang, by the way. Since we came clean – since I came clean – she seems to feel she ought to keep an eye on me. Quite frankly, it makes me feel all soppy. I'm getting vulnerable in my old age. Does she check up on you too?"

"Quite a lot."

"Bless her." Gazing out of the window, Zoe went on, "Eric, incidentally, married his girl. A few weeks ago. They're living happily ever after in Barnes. Don't gnash your teeth for me. Oddly enough, it's not quite as bad as I thought it would be. I've had a rather different slant on life lately which seems to have tempered the outlook."

"What slant, Zoe?"

"Nothing very original. Just a strong feeling that being around despite the perversities is a damn sight better than not being around. In the absence of any firm evidence of a life to come." She looked directly at Frances. "What you've always been very well aware of, love, until recently. Is there any hope that you might be beginning to feel that way again, at all?"

"Some days," said Frances, "I believe there is."

It had taken Morris two weeks of scouring sale rooms and antique shops to track down a sufficiently appealing picture of a dog. Dogs, he had decided, are not in themselves appealing; the presentation is all. And when at last he achieved a feathery spaniel creature brooding over a dead pheasant amid autumn leaves he anguished about whether it had period charm or was merely a cliché. In a state of dreadful anxiety he presented it to Frances, watching her face intently. He knew at once that it was all right.

"I thought it would be something you haven't got," he said modestly.

“I shall hang it over the mantelpiece. I’d been wondering what to have there.”

For the next half hour Morris tried to ask what he wanted to ask and retreated, each time, at the brink. At last he proposed that he should hang the picture for her and then, standing on a chair with his back to her, hammer in one hand and picture hook in the other, he got it out. At least her face wouldn’t tell him at once that this wasn’t all right.

“I gave to go to this festival in Canterbury the weekend after next. Baroque music, mainly. A couple of nights. I wondered if you might like to come with me.” He squinted in agonised suspense at the picture, his nose a few inches from the glossy painted nose of the dog – an artful dog, he now decided, an artful sycophantic dog, posing forever with its pheasant and its glistening anthropomorphic brown eyes. “Just an idea,” he said lightly (too lightly?) and heard Frances say, in a perfectly ordinary matter-of-fact tone that why yes, that sounded fun, she hadn’t anything on the weekend after next, yes, why not?

Frances, later, when he had gone, straightened the picture which had hung lop-sided ever since Morris, unsuccessfully simulating calm and nonchalance, had got down from the chair. She thought, in alarm, what have I done? what am I doing?

It was the middle of October. Frances, Zoe, Morris and Tabitha, all of whom spent a good part of their days sitting behind a desk, separately watched, through glass, the mutation of the year. They sat with books or papers or typewriters and looked up, every now and then, at skies that were sometimes serenely blue and sometimes loaded with rain. Each noted the onward rush of time and looked back at their own innocence of a year ago.

Frances measured the progress of her grief. Zoe thought, I am without Eric, but I am with Tab, and I am not ill. Morris thought, A year ago I knew nothing of her, I did not know she existed.

Tabitha, crunching around through the fallen leaves of Cambridge – was there ever a place so drowned in leaves? – thought about books. She had lived, she realised, ever since she could confidently read, through the pages of books. She had been Tess and Natasha and Catherine Earnshaw and the girl in *Rebecca* and later and more ambitiously Madame Bovary and Anna Karenina. She knew all about passion and suffering and the complexity of things. She had grown up in feverish pursuit of information, and there it all was, stacked away on the shelves. Accordingly she was prepared for anything; nothing could surely be either better or worse than the books said it would be.

She remembered, as a small child, rushing into a sea which had turned out to be quite startlingly wet and cold, its feel utterly unrelated to its look. The quilted surface and the delicately frilled waves had been lies – no, not lies but another dimension. And the books while not lying were similarly quite unconnected with the raw facts. They told you – oh dear me yes, they told you – but what they were telling you saw as through a glass, darkly. They could not explain the shocking truth that when someone you love dies they cease to be there any more in a way that is barely credible, or that happiness scarcely gives you time to know it for what it is or that unhappiness is pain.

Or that the past is overlaid by the present. She telephoned Zoe and said, "Do I look like him, at all?"

"Like who?"

"Him. The man. My, um, father."

"I don't think so," said Zoe, after a moment. "I'm pretty sure not. He was tall. You're stunted, like me."

"Small," said Tabitha.

"Petite, then." There was silence. "I'm sorry," Zoe went on. "You see I don't remember him very well." There was a further silence. "I feel . . . shabby."

"Don't," said Tabitha. "Please don't. I'd much rather you didn't. Anyway, it doesn't really matter."

The events of the summer were retreating. She began to see them as though down a tunnel, getting increasingly smaller, leaving only the flavours of joy and distress. She saw and did new things. The autumn days took her onwards with them.

Frances, through the window beside her desk at the Institute, could observe the building-site next door. It looked, at times, as complex and difficult to analyse as one of those teeming Italian paintings: a Calvary or a Rape of the Sabines or Massacre of the Innocents. Men and machinery clambered around landscapes of rubble and timber structures that changed their form day by day, the men picked out by their brilliant yellow helmets, the trucks and bulldozers gaudily orange and red. Lakes appeared and disappeared. It was impossible to discern any kind of purpose. And then as the summer ended method emerged from the chaos: the random burrowing gave way to a forest of poles and girders, the skeleton of a huge building began to rise from the London soil. Frances and Patricia, for whom site-watching had become a compulsive occupation during their coffee and lunch breaks, felt a sense of personal achievement.

"When I'm an old woman," said Patricia, "I shall be able to say I knew that block when it was nothing."

They had formed a comfortable relationship. A few days before Patricia had said briskly, "How do you feel about staying on permanently? If it suits you, it suits me. I've already had a word with the Director." Frances replied, "Thank you. I'd like to."

That night, lying in bed, she was filled with cautious pleasure. I have occupation, she thought. I am not indispensable but modestly useful; I have made myself a home, of a kind; I have friends who never knew Steven. I am moving on.

She had been sent the list of those to be invited to the memorial lecture, with a note from the chairman of the committee asking her to make any further suggestions she thought proper. She read through the columns of names and added Steven's mother and her own, knowing that neither would come but that both would derive a small vicarious glory. Several people were included, she noticed, who had been official enemies of Steven's; she wondered if she was allowed also to make deletions. That would cause an interesting stir. Shall I? she said to him, with a glint. And remembered an occasion when one of these same people had come up to them in a street somewhere, greeting Steven with effusive and apparently unfeigned warmth. He had been infuriated; "What's the world coming to when you can't even rely on your enemies?" She sat smiling, the list in her hand.

Zoe went to Kew Gardens, alone. She walked among the flaming trees and marvelled. She studied the little metal plaques attached to them and wrote down names, deriding at the same time the professional tic that made her do this. For Christ's sake, she said to herself, you rush through life with your head down writing it up and then you come here and do the same. She dropped the notebook into a litter bin and walked on, looking at trees graceful and trees majestic and trees that smouldered like candles. I know nothing about vegetation, she thought. You move around the world and know nothing of it. I will get a book about botany and I will learn Italian at last, I swear it. And I'll take a holiday.

On the morning that Frances was to meet Morris at Charing Cross for the train to Canterbury she re-packed her case twice, seized with nervousness that took the form of distaste for all her clothes. She put things in and then took them out again and then searched frantically for a garment that seemed suddenly indispensible and thus kept the taxi waiting five minutes and departed breathlessly, grabbing the letters from the hall table as she went. Glancing through them she found a card from Ruth Bowers: 'I find myself with an unexpected assignment to a librarians' conference in your city next week. I'll take you up on your invitation to visit, if I may. Will call you on . . .' The date was illegible. Frances thrust the card into her pocket. Good, she thought, I shall like to see her again.

Morris was at the barrier. They were flung, immediately, into a disabling uneasiness and both began to talk at once.

"Sorry I'm late. You must have thought I was going to miss the train. I wonder if there are any seats left."

"Let me take your case. It looks as though the weather's going to be good, anyway. There's a buffet car, I see."

They walked self-consciously down the platform. Morris said, "Do you know Canterbury at all?"

Frances stopped. She faced him. "I've been looking forward to this so much, Morris."

He beamed. "Have you? That's all right, then. I certainly have. I was so excited this morning I couldn't eat any breakfast."

Frances laughed. She took his arm. "We'd better get somewhere near this buffet car, in that case."

In the train, Morris said, "Two concerts are musts. For me, at any rate. For the rest of the time we do exactly what we like."

"I shall go to everything you're going to."

The train rocked through the fields and woods: the tranquil somehow old-fashioned southern English landscape that bore still a whiff of those thirties railway posters, as though busty girl hikers in shorts should appear on a skyline, or the white-painted stations offer Cream Teas. They sat side by side and did not talk all the time; Frances read the newspaper and Morris a book he was reviewing. She thought, startled; to others we presumably look like a married couple. Long-married, given our ages.

At the hotel reception desk they were seized again with awkwardness. "I've booked two rooms," said Morris. "Of course."

"Yes," said Frances. "Thank you," she added, foolishly.

They went to the Festival Office for Morris to collect tickets and brochures. The town was brandishing the occasion with pride: there were posters all over the place. "Tonight the English Chamber Orchestra in the cathedral," said Morris. "Tomorrow the LSO. For now – a general potter around?"

In the train, and standing with him in her hotel room, pointing out the distant view of the cathedral towers, Frances had been filled with a sense of physical proximity which was partly sexual and partly something else. They seemed, both of them, intensely there: hands and eyes and hair and the ring of footsteps and movement of limbs. Entering the cathedral, passing from the bright gusty outside into that still and sober height all this suddenly fell away. It was as though they, and everyone else, shrank and faded. People drifted about looking upwards, not at each other. Frances, after a few minutes, realised that she had lost Morris; she came upon him at last in the choir, poring over the guide-book. She was gripped by a wave of affection and relief, as when one struggles through anonymous crowds to find the familiar face at a rendezvous. Although she had lived in a city much of her life it never ceased to surprise her that we move, most of the time, among people we have never seen before and will never see again. Occasionally, this had given her a curious sense of panic. Here, though, the way in which the cathedral drained individuals of significance and made one feel oneself impersonal was somehow satisfying. Morris's known face, though, shone for her. She went up and laid a hand on his arm. He began to read her extracts from the guide-book: the fire, the re-building, the use of Purbeck marble. "Do you want to hear all this? Some people prefer just looking?"

"Go on," she said. "I want to hear." It came to her that he was doing just what Steven would have done; she tried to drive the thought away. Morris said, "The crypt, I think, is the next thing. Solid Norman, apparently, and considered one of the best." She followed him down the steps.

Secrecy supplanted space: the secrecies of mysterious and incommunicable mythologies. Frances, looking along the squat ranks of piers, at the vaulted roof, thought; even the air here is different. She examined the strange inhuman faces on the capitals, man-beast mutations, malevolent serpentine heads, and then glanced at Morris, at an elderly man with a camera, squinting upwards, at a little girl in a pink dress. Here we are, she thought, all flesh and feeling in the middle of this dead stone and cold thick air, a place beyond grief or pleasure. She said to Morris, "It feels hostile."

He looked at her, with a slight frown. "How?"

"Because it is beyond everything. Outside time altogether."

"We'll go," he said solicitously, "if it makes you uncomfortable."

"Not uncomfortable, really. Just out of place."

They walked in the cloister. Frances said, "I'm flagging, I shall have to have a rest." She sat on the stone wall, in sunshine, leaning against a column. She could feel, without turning her head, Morris looking at her; his gaze lay on her face, warm. She moved her head and smiled. Morris said, "What is unthinkable is that this weekend has to come to an end."

"Then don't think it." She stood up. "Let's go and have some lunch."

Morris thought, I shall never be able to come to this place again. Whatever happens between us. For ever after this pleasant Kentish town will be hallowed. Or tainted, as the case may be. Even cathedrals, he realised a little wildly, might be insecure. For ever after, in the dim calm light of naves and choirs, he would see Frances's fair head tilted upwards, inspecting capitals and vaulting.

And the day did not slip from his fingers, as he had feared, but most beautifully expanded. It went on and on. It became, in some miraculous way, time apart; a different quality of time. There was the time in the cathedral and the time eating lunch in the rather crowded pub at the end of the High Street and the time wandering in the afternoon around the bookshops and the cathedral precinct and the garden in which roses so exuberantly bloomed. The time back at the hotel, bathing and changing for dinner, when he came to fetch Frances and found her not yet ready, and sat entranced on the bed while she did her hair and sought out the shoes she needed, and the necklace. The time back in the cathedral, at the concert. The time afterwards, having dinner. Each of which was different: times of gaiety and times of sobriety and times of intimacy and times when distantly, almost beyond awareness, sadness lurked. 'In the midst of life we are in death,' said an inscription in the cathedral; Morris, noting it, had thought: no, not death, just change, instability, the flight of things.

And now there was the time at the end of this day, when he found all of a sudden that in fact the nervous rehearsed scenarios dissolved, were inappropriate and unnecessary and in fact what should be said and done arrived quite naturally, without thought or consideration. He came to her room and he put his arms round her and they took their clothes off and went to bed and made love. In the middle of it all he looked down at her and said, "You're not just doing this to be polite, are you?" And she had smiled. Smiled and said nothing in reply but simply lain there beneath him and around him; this pleasure, he saw and he felt, was shared.

It was much later, in the cold small hours, that Morris woke and realised, almost dispassionately, that Frances did not love him and perhaps never would.

Chapter Sixteen

Frances and Zoe, ushered to the front row of the lecture hall, found themselves flanked by the Director and various academic household names. Patricia Geering, in what Frances now knew to be her best dress, stood in the aisle, discreetly allocating seats. She and Frances exchanged private smiles. Zoe, periodically, turned round and stared backwards into the hall, reporting loudly on the size of the audience and faces she recognised. The Director eyed her nervously, as though she were some unstable substance. Zoe, observing this, whispered to Frances, "I'm the sort of woman who scares the pants off that sort of man. They wait to be set upon." "Hush," said Frances. "I work here." "All right, all right."

The lecturer arrived and took his place at the lectern. He stood for a few moments sorting out his papers, an elderly pear-shaped man with silver-rimmed spectacles that were, throughout the lecture, to shunt slowly down his nose and be swept up again in the nick of time by his adroit left forefinger. He began to speak – of his appreciation at being invited to deliver this lecture, of Steven. He paid tribute to Steven's work. Frances wondered if Steven had known him; the man's name was unfamiliar to her. He was considerably older than Steven; his presence, and Steven's absence, seemed an affront. She gazed at him, trying to suppress this feeling, trying to pay attention to his lecture, which was about German re-armament after the First World War. It was a depressing theme; the burden of the argument was that intensive accumulation of military hardware had always culminated in war and would always do so. The lecture over, she said to Zoe, "Gloomy stuff."

"That's not the only kind of history. The prophetic past. There are more optimistic approaches."

The Director, now, was leading the lecturer down from the platform and towards them. "Mrs Brooklyn. Miss Brooklyn. Professor Harrington." They stood for a moment; the professor believed that he and Frances had briefly met once some years ago in, um, Manchester. He had appreciated Zoe's article on the American gun laws. The Director suggested they should move through to the Common Room. "I could certainly use a drink," said Zoe, in an insufficiently muted voice. The back of the Director's neck, ahead of them, seemed to curdle slightly.

The room filled up. Frances, engaged by Harrington, stood listening to an account of a recent visit to China. It should have been interesting but wasn't. Zoe, more adroit at escape, had already slid away; Frances could see her head bobbing between people's shoulders as she cruised in search of someone more enlivening to talk to. Just, she thought, what Steven would have done. But here am I, too polite or too inert to do anything but stand here nodding occasionally. With a pleasant flood of warmth Morris's voice came to her: "You're not just doing this to be polite, are you?" Needing to know. And no, she thought, I wasn't, I most certainly wasn't.

Over the professor's shoulder she could see faces framed by backs and other shoulders. This was a good deal more interesting than the professor's discourse since, she gradually perceived, many of these faces were known faces and formed a curious kaleidoscope of reminder. Over there was a college friend of Steven's who had been at their wedding; his grey hair startled her for a moment, as though there were something wrong with him. And there was the man who had once so ineptly told her in Stockholm that she would have to wait her turn, now, for Steven's attention; a differently emotive presence. There was the woman who had been Steven's personal assistant at the College for the last two years and there were other colleagues and ex-colleagues and friends and foes: a patchwork of associations, each face prompting a series of quickly vanishing slides: the time when she had been at this place, done such-and-such, when this or that had been said. She gazed, intrigued, quite deaf now to Harrington, who was in Peking shrewdly analysing the significance of an infant school; she did not particularly want to go and talk to any of these people, indeed the prospect was disheartening, but the sight of them, thus gathered together in this one room, was oddly compelling. As though some private photograph album had been brought to life.

A momentary parting of bodies revealed Zoe, in animated conversation with an unidentifiable back. She raised a hand, waved, beckoned.

"Excuse me," said Frances. "My sister-in-law . . . I think she wants . . . I'm sure I'll see you again before we go." She smiled placatingly, and began to edge across the room, Zoe now engulfed again by the crowd.

She was halted, almost at once, by the man from the Stockholm conference, keen to recall what, in his terms, appeared to be some quite different occasion. She endured this with mounting resentment, trapped again. She couldn't be bothered to dispute his version. When he offered to get her a drink she accepted and then, guiltily, moved onwards, only to find herself blocked by a group which at once absorbed her. "Ah," said the Director, "Frances . . . I want you to meet, um . . ." And this man, it emerged, had been associated with Steven at some point, somewhere, and after initial token reticence was keen to describe a trip they had taken to Washington together in, er . . . "Nineteen seventy," said Frances. "Of course. The occasion being the Senate's invitation to . . ." Yes, thought Frances, I know too, he was gone over three weeks and I missed him like hell and was so pleased when he got back that I started snapping at him in the taxi from Heathrow. She felt dragged down by all this and wished she hadn't come. Zoe seemed to have disappeared completely. I should have said no, she thought, or at least said no to this junket, just gone to the lecture. But that would have been taken for inability to face up to things, cowardice of some kind, which in a way is exactly what it would have been. Except that renewed grief is not what this is bringing on, but something else entirely.

I must not, she thought with sudden clarity, be forever hitched to what has been. Only to such of it as I choose, to such of it that will sustain me.

The man stopped remembering Washington. Someone else broke in with a remark. Frances, discovering a new opportunism, moved away.

A voice said, "You're Frances Brooklyn, aren't you?"

She was a tall woman with dark hair, middle-aged. Her tone stated a fact rather than invited confirmation; it lacked, also, warmth.

Frances said, "Yes."

"My name's Sarah Hennings. I knew Steven rather well a very long time ago."

There was a silence. "Yes," said Frances. "I know."

"I daresay he talked about me. We were engaged for a bit."

Frances could think only: how did she get here? Sarah Hennings, uncannily, smiled, "So I thought I'd come along. Out of a kind of sentiment. It's a public lecture, after all. And then when I saw everyone coming in here I thought one extra wouldn't be noticed. And I wanted to meet you."

"Yes," said Frances again. "I see. Well . . ." She couldn't think of anything to say. Sarah Hennings had large, slightly protuberant eyes which were in the process of examining her, with detachment and, she felt, not a great deal of charity.

"Of course my name isn't still Hennings strictly speaking, though I do use it at work. It's Creighton really. My husband's a senior lecturer at Brunel. He's never risen to Steven's dizzy heights professionally." She contemplated Frances. "I suppose you've had to get out of that gorgeous house. I drove past it once – someone told me you lived there."

Frances gazed in amazement. "Yes, I'm living somewhere else now. Out of choice."

"Really?" said Sarah Hennings. "Didn't you go for all those official trappings? I've often thought what fun it must be. I enjoy entertaining, personally. Not that Brunel offers much scope. I suppose you went all over the place with Steven?"

"Not often. I'm not all that addicted to travel. And there were the children."

"I would have done. I remember reading in the paper once that he was off to Russia on some international whatsit and I thought some people have all the luck."

"Actually," said Frances, "he didn't want to go that much. He was very busy at the time."

"I was thinking of you, not him. Getting a free ride to Moscow."

Frances silenced, could only stare. This is insane, she thought, this woman I never heard of until a month ago has been watching me for years.

"He'd have got a K, I suppose, in a year or two."

"A what?" said Frances.

"A K. A knighthood. Sir Steven. And Lady."

"I've no idea," said Frances, enraged.

"I always watched when he was on the box. Interesting. I s'pose you went to TV parties and met all those glamorous people."

"No."

Sarah Hennings glanced over Frances's shoulder. "You must know everyone here."

"Some of them."

"I work in PR. For a publisher. Which slightly mitigates Brunel. Well, it's all a long time ago now, but I must say I've always stayed interested, in a funny way."

"What's a long time ago?" enquired Frances.

"When I knew Steven. It didn't work out, of course. Otherwise . . ." Sarah Hennings laughed, "Otherwise I s'pose it would have been me larking off to Washington and places, and living it up in super houses. No – we were awfully fond of each other for a bit but we kind of mutually agreed that it wouldn't work out. You've got two children, haven't you?"

Frances took a deep breath. Somewhere in the depths of this person, she thought, there lurks the remnant of a girl who was sufficiently different for her once to have been someone Steven liked. Loved, for a while, I suppose. And she does not matter to me in the least, not in the very least, so I must stay calm and not say or do or feel any of the things I . . .

"So have we. Deep into adolescence now. Yours are adopted, aren't they? I remember somebody saying once. You must miss him dreadfully. It must seem awfully kind of empty, I imagine. If you ever feel like an evening in Uxbridge give us a ring. Didn't Steven's parents use to live somewhere that way?"

Frances looked round wildly. Zoe was nowhere to be seen. The room had thinned out a little; people were beginning to leave. Her head ached and she had a sense of creeping disorientation. All she could think was: I knew I shouldn't have come.

"Actually," said Sarah Hennings. "You look rather done in. I imagine this sort of thing is a bit of a strain." She glanced sideways, "That's Lord Briggs, isn't it. I suppose you know him?"

Frances said, "I have to have a word with the Director before I go." I cannot, she thought, say even the anodyne and meaningless things. I am not so glad to have met you.

Sarah Hennings shifted the strap of her handbag further on to her shoulder. "I'm off too. Well, I'm glad I've seen you. Actually I did once years ago, at a distance. You and Steven were at some theatre. You had a blue and green Liberty silk dress. I remember thinking nice and pricey. Anyway . . . 'Bye."

"Goodbye," said Frances.

And now, too late, here was Zoe advancing across the room, appearing from nowhere, beaming, saying, "Hi . . . *There* you are. Hey, guess who I've been talking to." She glanced at Sarah Hennings' departing back. "Who was that?"

"Just someone Steven knew," said Frances. "Inevitably. I want to go home."

She should have talked to Zoe, but she could not. She sat silent in the taxi and Zoe chattered on and, at the corner of Frances's street they kissed and Zoe was borne away into the night. She felt for her keys and unlocked the door and went into the black and empty house. She switched on the hall light and then the sitting room one and it was bright but continuously empty. She took off her coat and sat down on the sofa and there was nothing to be heard but the tick of the hall clock and the whisper of a passing car. She experienced, all at once, each of the miseries of the past year: grief and loneliness and, above all, that fracturing of the mind she had known in Venice. It was like the sudden onset of the old familiar pain in an invalid who has been groping towards health. She thought, I must not be alone. And then, almost immediately, I need not be alone. She sat looking at the telephone. She could pick it up and dial the number and she could speak to Morris. He would be there, in all likelihood, at this time of the evening. They could talk and she would not be alone any more. Probably – certainly – he would come if she wished. The house would no longer be continuously empty.

And she knew, even as she thought all this, that she would not do it. I will not take advantage, she thought, of a man who I'm afraid feels more for me than I think I will ever feel for him. I dearly wish it were otherwise, but that is how it is and for that reason I cannot and will not pick up that telephone and make use of him. I shall go through this on my own, as I have all along.

The telephone rang.

She sat looking at it, in alarm.

She picked it up, at last, and said, "Yes?"

"Is that Frances? This is Ruth Bowers here."

"Ruth!" she exclaimed, "You're in London! But of course – your postcard. Only I didn't know exactly when . . . I couldn't read the date. It's very good to hear you."

Ruth was saying, "And how are *you*? . . . I called you earlier, I couldn't figure out what I should do, I thought maybe you were out of town . . ." "How are you?" she said again. That brisk slightly harsh voice; the voice of goodness and sanity and time was – not so much time, either – salvation.

Frances said, "I have been well. Really quite well. Just at this moment I'm feeling rather low, I'm afraid."

There was a pause. "How about me dropping over and visiting for a while?" said Ruth. "If it's not too late for you, it's not too late for me."

They sat on the sitting room sofa eating scrambled eggs. The bottle of red wine was half empty. Ruth Bowers said,

"This is the nearest I've got in years to being back in the dormitory in college." She shook, suddenly, with laughter. "Hey – will you look at the time! I guess I will take up that offer of your spare bed. My hotel will think I'm having a night on the tiles."

Frances said, "You seem fated to arrive in time to pick up the pieces, where I'm concerned."

Ruth patted her arm. "But you're going to be O.K. now, right?"

"I think so. Yes, I'm sure I will."

"This won't be the last bad day. But I guess each time you'll get a bit better at it. You know something – I'd say your Steven gave that lady the push, way back, never mind all that stuff about mutually agreeing."

"Maybe," said Frances. "In fact I daresay that's right. It wasn't so much her that upset me – I was more upset the first time I realised about her – as this feeling that someone you didn't even know had been eyeing you, for years."

"Frances," said Ruth. "There's an awful lot of people in this world feel the grass somewhere else is greener. Your Steven was the green grass she didn't have."

"Not him, really. What went with him."

Ruth yawned. "If you'll excuse me, Frances, I'll borrow that nightdress and go to bed. We have our big day tomorrow and I have to chair one of the sessions."

"It was good of you to come over, Ruth. I was feeling very . . . precarious. Thank you."

Ruth patted her arm again. "A pleasure. Tell you something – Thursday we get our free day and a tour of Blenheim Palace and

Stratford upon Avon I can do without. Why don't we have a private day out?"

"That will be my pleasure," said Frances.

A few miles away, sharing nothing with her but the hour, separated by space and by what he felt, Morris lay thinking of Frances. Or rather, since thought implies deliberation, he lay in awareness of Frances. He would have preferred, in fact, to do otherwise, but had no choice. She filled the darkness around his bed, inducing feelings so assorted that he had long since lost track of whether pleasure predominated, or distress. He savoured those hours in Canterbury, again and again; he sat once more in the park with her hand in his; he basked in the warmth of her look. He wondered, protectively, how she had fared at the lecture and the reception. It may be a bit of an ordeal, she had said in the train from Canterbury. And so, all day, he had thought of this; late in the evening he had itched to telephone her, but had resisted, fearing to intrude.

He switched on the light. It was three in the morning. He went to the kitchen, made himself a cup of tea and took it into the living room. He stood for a moment in front of a pile of records on which he had to write an article and placed one on the turntable. But almost at once he took it off, searched along his record cabinet and found the fifth Brandenburg Concerto. Do your worst, he said to it.

And indeed the music invoked that occasion when first he saw her, but what it also brought as he sat there in the middle of the solitary city night was the recognition that in all beginnings, stealthy and unnoticed, lurking like the pod amid the petals, are their endings. Every moment has spawned already all its descendants and there is nothing to be done.

It is not ended, he thought. She likes me and she liked going to bed with me and I shall see her again. But I shall not, because of what I now fear would be said in return, ever say to her the things I hoped to say. At least not now and perhaps never. I don't think that she will ever marry me or come to live with me.

And, even as he thought this, resistance softly but stubbornly flamed. But I may be wrong. I do not know. We none of us know. It is not knowing that makes it all endurable.

Frances, Zoe and Tabitha, some weeks later, on a grey afternoon at the dark end of the year, in November, in Cambridge, listen also to music. Not Brandenburg Five but Bartok which Tabitha, who is playing as well as listening, finds tricky. She peers at the score and occasionally is obliged to do some dexterous improvisation (I must practise more, she tells herself sternly) but she is swept along with the rest of them, bar by bar and movement by movement, beginning to end.

Frances and Zoe separately contemplate those impervious faces walled up in their gilt frames and their unimaginable times, those other live and intent faces of the musicians, and the fragile daylight that comes down through the windows. Last time they were here those shafts had been the robust yellow sunshine of early summer and both, independently, note this.

Zoe looks at Tabitha, who is as she was then and also subtly different. I need you, she thinks, I am going to need you, though I will never let on, being the obstinate cuss that I am. We are both older and wiser than when we were last in this room.

Especially I, who thought I had done all the learning and changing I ever would.

Five months, thinks Frances. Onward by five months. Onward and outward. And where have they brought me? She considers, sitting there with her hands folded in her lap and the music carrying her with it. Not out of grief but into a state in which, eventually, I can live. Which I have made for myself, out of the past and out of a future that I begin to be able to look at. I am hitched, again, to time and to the world.

Later, she drove into London, alone. The city gathered around her as she penetrated it, the houses and shops closing ranks, the traffic slowing and thickening. The grey wintry afternoon was jewelled with lights, green and red and amber in a brilliant avenue ahead all the way down the streets. When she reached her own part it was almost night; the long perspectives of the terraces gleamed pale behind the wrought-iron precision of bare trees and the sudden brilliant flare of street-lamps. The tail-lights of cars glowed, piling up ahead in a bank of colour. An office-block soared into the sky like an incandescent bar and the sky itself was orange, not sky but an extension of what lay beneath, a huge wild reflection of the city. She thought it beautiful, and was quietly exhilarated, as though this were some private vision. She drove towards her house, neither happy nor grieving, looking not backwards into the day but on into the next.